Second Love After 50

Lilly Setterdahl

Lilly Setterdahl

The royalty-free cover photo was purchased from
canstock.com

Second Love After 50
All rights reserved

Chapter 1

Andrea Holm cruised along the Interstate with ease as the Chicago suburbs shrank in her rearview mirror and the sun rose higher behind her. Ahead, the sundrenched prairieland stretched unbroken to the western horizon. At the sight of its rich, black soil ready for planting, she felt embraced by the promise of spring. Josh Groban's melodious voice filled the car with words of love, adding to the vague sensation of hope and new beginnings.

Andrea had been a widow for two years after 28 years of marriage, and the loneliness seemed unbearable at times. Still, she hoped to avoid taking on the bitterness that had become the way of life for many lonely women.

She smiled wryly. The hope of spring? New beginnings? Where would those sentiments fit into her life as a 52-year-old widow with a fulltime job and an elderly mother? Andrea loved her mother and didn't begrudge the 90-minute drive to visit her, but why couldn't her sisters do it once in a while?

Nana, as everyone in the family called her, could drive to visit Andrea, but she wouldn't attempt to drive in the Chicago traffic all the way to the north shore to visit her other two daughters, Kathy and Nancy.

Dear Nana, you deserve visits from all of us, but I'm the only one you can count on. Besides, you need some help in your home once in awhile.

Kathy, I love you, but your boys are teenagers now. I know you do volunteer work, but I don't hear you volunteering to visit Nana.

Nancy, I love you too, but why can't you take your girls with you and go to Nana's house on a weekend? Just because I'm alone, I shouldn't be expected to do all the visiting.

I'm doing it again, feeling sorry for myself.

Andrea made a face at her rearview image and took stock of her situation. Flipping her auburn hair over her shoulder, she tried not to think about her need for a haircut and the hours she put in at the bookstore that prevented her from making an appointment. I should think about all the positive things in my life.

I'm healthy. My family loves me. I adore my mother and daughter. I'm lucky to have them in my life. I enjoy assisting my customers at the store in their search for the right book. I get along with my coworkers, and I do have good friends although they are not as many as when my husband was alive.

I'm not perfect. Sometimes my anger flares and I get defensive. But most people say that I'm kind and friendly. I can still draw admiring looks from men. I really have many positives in my life—except a man to love.

Low, dark clouds in the distance drew Andrea's attention back to driving. She was heading in the direction of the rain. The sudden change in the weather was no surprise to her. After all, she lived in the Midwest, but as the black clouds came closer, the imminent threat of a severe storm filled her with unease.

By the time she had popped Josh out of the CD player and fumbled to find a weather forecast on the radio, the morning had turned evening dark. Lightning flashed and thunder crackled. Rain beat on the car. The wipers and the headlights helped but not much. She could hardly see the road.

Before she knew it, lightning pierced the sky. A loud thunderbolt made her jump in her seat. In the same instant, a streak of lightning struck a corncrib, and it erupted in flames. It frightened her enough to slow down.

The wind increased and the torrential rain blinded her. She saw the headlights of two cars behind her. Andrea took her foot off the accelerator and signaled to turn to the shoulder of the road and stop, but it was too late.

She felt a hard jolt and heard the crash of metal. Her car lurched forward. "Oh, my God!" The sharp pain in her chest and neck made her scream.

Moments later, a man stood outside her car and motioned to her to roll down her window. When she finally did, he said, "I've called 911. Are you hurt, ma'am?" Andrea was in too much pain to answer. She pointed to her chest and neck and moaned. Her body shook.

The man said something about a three-vehicle crash. She remembered the two cars behind her. The cars that swished by splashed water on the man outside. She couldn't find her voice so she motioned to him to come and sit beside her. He said he would be back, but first he had to check on the driver in the third car.

The man had wet, gray hair plastered to his skull. Andrea's eyes followed him in the side-view mirror as he walked away. His shoulders slumped, one more than the other.

The pain in her chest was almost unbearable. The thunder roared and the rain intensified. The trees swayed in the wind. When the man returned, he had trouble walking upright against the wind. He pulled hard on her right door to open it. Everything added to Andrea's anguish.

"My car is a wreck, and so am I," she thought.

"I'm sorry you're hurt, ma'am. You must be frightened," the man said as he climbed into the passenger seat. Listening to his kind words made her cry. Weakness overcame her. She tried to wet her lips, but her mouth felt dry as sandpaper. Her breath was fast and shallow.

"I can't, I can't turn my head." Her voice sounded like a child's.

"It's okay." He paused before introducing himself. "I'm Charles Bordeaux," his voice deep and steady.

Andrea stammered her name. "Andrea... Andrea Holm. What happened?"

"A pickup rear-ended my vehicle. I saw your turn signal ahead and tried to avoid you, but everything happened so fast."

He said vehicle. It sounds so professional. If only I could turn my head and look at him? He's so polite.

Andrea tried hard to conceal her pain. She was regaining her composure. "How come you aren't hurt?"

"My airbag inflated. It hurt my chest but I'll be fine."

Airbag, she had airbags, why didn't hers inflate.

"The young driver who hit me was alone in his vehicle. He seemed dazed and didn't answer me when I asked if he was hurt. Someone else stopped to aid him."

Andrea shuddered at the thought of the young man being badly hurt. The seatbelt held her fast. It was an awful, almost suffocating feeling.

"We're lucky to be alive," she mumbled.

"Indeed we are."

His modulated speech made her think he was a professional of some kind.

What was his name? Charles Bordeaux. It sounds French. I wish I could see him.

"They'll probably take you to the hospital in DeKalb? It's the closest. I'll try to check on you there, but my car is not operational. It's damaged in both the front and back."

She hung onto every word he said. It took her mind off her pain. When he asked her where she was from, she said Naperville. He said that he lived in a rural area to the north.

They heard the emergency sirens before they saw the police car and the paramedic unit.

Before Charles stepped out to talk with the police, he turned to Andrea and said, "My contact information will be in the police report and so will yours in case you want to keep in touch, Miss Holm."

The rain had stopped and the sun came out of the clouds.

A paramedic opened her door. "Ma'am, are you hurt?" he asked.

"She pointed to her chest and neck. "I'm stuck," she croaked.

"Don't worry. We'll get you out, ma'am."

The paramedic unsnapped her seatbelt and moved her seat as far back as he could. Another man from the ambulance wrapped a brace around her neck before lifting her out and placing her on a stretcher. She clutched her chest in pain and moaned.

"Does your chest hurt, ma'am?"

Andrea nodded. The paramedic checked her pulse and made a phone call. "We're bringing in a middle-aged female complaining of chest pain," he said.

He was talking about her, a middle-aged female. Oh, my God! She could almost see the headline in the paper.

Am I having a heart attack? Will I die? I'm scared. Where did Charles go?

She was on the verge of losing it when Charles appeared at her side.

"You'll be all right," he said. In the sunlight, she saw that his eyes were blue and that he had a cleft in his chin. The sight of him calmed her, but she was still frightened.

The cool April air felt refreshing after the rain and it helped her think more clearly, but the noise and the bustle around her bothered her. How many people were hurt? She saw another ambulance. The running engines sent fumes her way. A tow truck took away her Ford Escort that looked badly damaged in the rear. Charles saw it, too. He no longer wore his jacket, and his shirt was wet.

"You must be cold," Andrea said to him. She felt bad about having complained. The accident had hurt his chest and he was out there walking and showing his concern for others.

"I'll get some dry clothes from my car in a moment," he said, "if I can get to them?"

Their eyes focused on another truck towing a wreck.

"It's my car. It's a total loss," Charles said.

"How could you get out alive from that wreck?"

"I ask myself the same question," he said. He looked wistfully at the wreck, shrugged, and said, "There goes my dry shirt."

When a police officer came to talk to her, Charles stepped aside.

"Are these your belongings, ma'am?" the officer asked. When Andrea nodded, he put the purse by her side on the stretcher and the overnight bag by her feet.

He asked her many tiring questions. Andrea told him about the accident the best she could and was careful not to blame Charles. She was strapped to a stretcher and could hardly move. She had to show her license and proof of insurance. With difficulty, she removed the cards from her purse and handed them to the officer.

"Is this your current address, Miss Holm?"

"Yes." She gave the officer her phone numbers, and he wrote his report and gave her a copy. She would look at it later.

Charles stood a few feet away as she fingered her cell phone. Her hands were still a little shaky. She was going to call her mother, but didn't want to lose contact with Charles.

"Thank you for staying with me," she told him.

"Hope to see you again. Have a speedy recovery," he said as he raised one arm and waved to her. She feebly raised one hand.

As soon as she was in the ambulance, the paramedic brought out his stethoscope.

"Am I having a heart attack?" she asked. "It hurts to breathe."

He listened to her heart, and said, "No, ma'am. You've probably cracked a few ribs."

What a relief. She was too young to die.

"Your blood pressure is a little high, but it can be expected," he said. He asked about allergies and gave her two aspirin.

"The board underneath me is so hard," she said. "It hurts almost as much as my chest."

"We know, but we've to keep it there until we get to the hospital."

He asked her more questions, the current date, and the day of the week. It was April 3, 2005.

Andrea still wanted to call her mother, but it had to wait. Now, she was weary and tired from the shock and pain.

The ambulance started up. When it hit the bumps in the road, she groaned with pain.

Sorry, Nana, I can't come to see you.

I must think about something pleasant.

She closed her eyes and recalled the good times she and her sisters had spent at Nana's childhood farm with horses, cows, little calves, and newly hatched chicks. Those were precious memories. The location of the farm was not far from where she was now.

Her *mormor* and *morfar*, as she had called her mother's parents, were immigrants from Sweden. She remembered their accents and a few Swedish words she had learned as a child, like *tack så mycket* and *varsågod,* which meant thank you very much and please.

Mormor had taught them to say grace in Swedish and an evening prayer for children. After that, Nana had read the evening prayer with them every night while they were still small. Andrea couldn't think of the words now, but it was something about happiness comes and happiness goes, which was certainly true in her life.

Chapter 2

The emergency doctor on duty at the hospital listened to her heart and lungs and asked where it hurt. He said they needed x-rays. "The shoulder belt can hurt a person, especially a small woman like you," he said. Andrea swallowed a painkiller, but moaned every time they moved her. A nurse hooked her up to an IV.

After the x-rays, she was exhausted and fell asleep in the examination room. She dreamt about Philip, her late husband. He had come to her in a dream and kissed her with passion. Did he know that she needed him? She missed him so much. When they were married, they had promised to forsake all others as long they both lived, and they had lived up to their vow, but Philip was no longer alive. Was he trying to tell her something in her dream?

Damn it, Phil! You should be here.

Her anger surprised her.

Andrea's cell phone rang. Where was she? She sensed the bright lights and the smell of a hospital. The medication had made her groggy. She felt the pain in her chest and the stiffness in her neck as she reached for her purse to pull out her phone.

"Hello, Miss Holm. Are they treating you well?" She recognized Charles' voice right away. It was good to hear it again, but how did he get her number? Oh, it was in the police report.

"Yes, but I'm stiff as a board," she said in a horse voice.

"I know how you feel, because I'm getting stiffer by the minute."

Andrea managed a small smile.

"How did you get home, Mr. Bordeaux?"

"My eldest son who lives in DeKalb took me home. I'm glad to be alive, but my car's dead for sure."

Andrea again managed a slight smile in response to his remark.

"Do you have someone to take you home, Miss Holm?"

"Yes, my daughter. Oh, I have to call her, but first I need to call my mother. She's expecting me. I was on my way to see her."

"Then I'll hang up so you can call her. She'll be worried about you."

Andrea's hands shook as she speed-dialed her mother. It was good to hear her voice. Nana was the one presence in her life that had not changed.

"Sorry, I'm late, Nana." It brought relief to unburden herself as she explained what had happened. Nana offered to come to the hospital at once. Andrea protested, saying that Jessica could take her home, but Nana insisted. "I'd rather do something than sitting here worrying about you," she said.

"Drive carefully," Andrea said, but Nana had already hung up the phone.

I hope she takes the back roads as usual and not the Interstate. Here I've been worried that Nana would get in an accident on the road, and now I've been in one. It's so strange, but now I need her more than she needs me. Our roles have reversed.

Just thinking about her situation made Andrea cry.

The doctor came and talked to her. He said that her injuries were limited to a few fractured ribs and whiplash. "We'll be sending you home to recuperate," he said. He wrote a prescription and handed it to her, saying, "You'll have to wear a neck brace except at night. The icepack that we're sending home with you should ease some of the pain. Leave it on for 20 minutes at the time. You should see your own doctor as soon as possible."

Now that she was going home, Andrea grabbed her phone and pressed the number to her daughter, Jessica. While listening to the signal, she thought of her only child. She had the same Nordic look as her father, tall and blond with blue eyes. She had lived with Jason for a year now, and still no mention of marriage. They had good jobs. Jessica had accomplished her dream of becoming a schoolteacher.

Jessica answered the phone, and Andrea explained what had happened and that she was going home.

"Nana is on her way and she'll take me home."

"I could've come to get you, Mom," Jessica said.

"I know, but Nana insisted. I couldn't stop her before she hung up the phone. She has been to this hospital before, so I think she feels comfortable enough to drive here. You and Jason can meet us at home if you have time?"

"We'll come." If Jason can't come, I'll come."

It brought tears to Andrea's eyes. Thank God for mothers and daughters.

Her thoughts went to her own life. She still lived in the suburban home she had shared with her husband until two years ago when he died of cancer. Andrea blinked away tears as she thought of how hard it had been to lose Philip. He was so brave facing death.

She had cried for days after they learned that his disease was terminal. He said he was thankful for having seen their daughter grow up. It broke Andrea's heart to think that he would not be there for their future grandchildren.

When Phil was gone, she found out how hard it was to live without him. Their common friends called in the beginning, but soon stopped inviting her to parties. She had always selected his shirts, and now she couldn't stand seeing the store displays for men. The house felt empty and so did the king-sized bed they had shared. She replaced it with a smaller double bed, but it, too, felt empty. She twisted and turned at night.

Menopause didn't make it any easier. She perspired profusely and the next minute she was cold. Now, she was past that difficult time in her life and felt much better. Her part-time job at the bookstore had turned into a full-time position.

Andrea felt restrained. The slightest stir hurt. The pain had a grip on her upper body and neck. The hard, narrow gurney gave her no comfort. Finally, a nurse came and helped her sit up. Andrea braced herself against the pain. Her legs dangled while the nurse steadied her and wrapped her rib cage.

"Is someone coming for you?" the nurse asked.

"Yes, my mother, Margaret Chester."

"I'll remove the IV and help you to a wheelchair,"

Andrea's legs felt weak as the nurse helped her to stand up and get into the wheelchair. Her chest and neck still hurt. Scenes from the time Philip had been in the hospital played in her mind. She had pushed him in a wheelchair when he couldn't walk. She thought of her big, strong husband helpless in bed.

I want to get out of this place. I can't stand it. Where is Nana?

When Andrea saw her petite, gray-haired mother walking into the room, she smiled.

"I'm so glad to see you, Nana," she said. "Thanks for coming." Andrea fought back tears.

Her mother's clear blue eyes showed her concern as she asked about her injuries, and Andrea answered the best she could.

"I'm so sorry about this," Andrea said.

"Don't even mention it. I'm thankful that you're not seriously hurt."

Still, Andrea felt bad about needing her mother's help. The nurse began to wheel her out to the curb. She also had to help her get into the car and buckle the seatbelt. Overcome by weariness, Andrea fell asleep and didn't wake up until the car stopped outside her ranch house.

Jessica and Jason pulled up in the driveway behind them. Andrea heard their voices as they opened her car door, and felt Jessica's kiss on her cheek.

"You really scared us, Mom," Jessica said. There was deep concern in her young voice.

"I'm so terribly stiff. Sorry, I can't turn my head to look at you. I don't know how I'm going to get out of the car."

Jason intervened. "So sorry you're hurt, Andrea, but I'll help you," he said. His voice was strong and comforting. Carefully lifting her, he carried her in his arms. Jason was tall and muscular—a former football player. Andrea got a close look at his long, dark hair and grayish-blue eyes framed by thick, black eyelashes.

"I'll unlock the door for you," Jessica said.

"Where should I take you?" Jason asked.

"Front room, please."

Overcome by his kindness and her own weakness, she cried softly as Jason put her down on the couch. Perhaps it was the shock of it all. It was good to sit on something soft. The medication made her drowsy, but it was better than pain.

Nana brought out enough food for all of them and served it on trays in the living room. She said it was the dinner she had prepared for Andrea's visit. Andrea wasn't hungry, but she did her best to eat a little. Jason and Jessica devoured Nana's homemade Swedish cookies. After the meal, Andrea was glad to get into her own bed.

"I feel so helpless," she said to Jessica.

"It's only temporary, Mom. You'll get better in no time. Sorry, but we have to go now. Jason is waiting."

"Thank you both."

"I'll call you tomorrow, I love you, Mom."

Jason waved from the door opening.

"Thank you Jason for carrying me inside," Andrea said.

"No problem, hope you feel better soon," he replied.

Jessica's slim body and long legs looked good in the jeans she wore. Andrea was proud of her only child, and was glad that she had found someone to love. Jason was a good man.

Nana came and asked if she needed anything.

"I need my phone in case Charles Bordeaux calls."

"Who's he?"

"He's the man who hit me. He might call."

"Oh, I'll get your purse."

When Nana returned with the purse, Andrea asked her to bring the icepack. It was good to have Nana taking care of her. Just a couple of hours ago, she had been prepared to help Nana at her place.

Alone in her room, Andrea tried to remember what Charles Bordeaux looked like. She recalled his gray, wet hair, his blue eyes and the cleft in his chin.

Chapter 3

When Andrea awoke the next morning, scenes from the accident flashed in her mind as if she had hit a replay button. She felt the pain in her ribs and neck, but she also recalled a pair of blue eyes and the modulated, comforting voice of Charles Bordeaux. She couldn't turn her head to look at the clock. Instead, she called on her mother.

"Nana, can you please come here for a minute?"

Nana responded quickly. She'd been waiting for Andrea to wake up.

"How're you feeling today, honey?"

"I feel drowsy and stiff, but my pain is not as sharp as yesterday. What time is it?"

"It's nine o'clock, honey. Did you sleep well?"

"Thanks to the pills, but I feel awful and have to get up."

"I'll help you, but first I must put your brace back on."

It wasn't easy to get up, but supported by Nana, Andrea reached the bathroom. Looking in the mirror, she saw the big welt on the side of her neck that the seatbelt had made. Her breasts were bruised and so sore she couldn't touch them. Her hair hung in tangles around her face. She tried to brush it, but it was easier to use a big-tooth comb.

"I'm a mess," she said as she stumbled out of the bathroom.

"Honey, I could help you," Nana said.

"I must try to manage."

Andrea could smell the aroma of coffee as she touched the walls for support until she reached a chair in the kitchen. She heard her cell phone ring in the bedroom, and Nana hurried to get it, but when she handed the phone to Andrea, it had stopped ringing.

After breakfast, Andrea called the bookstore and told Bob, the manager, about the accident, saying she couldn't come to work for the next couple of weeks. Bob said he was sorry to hear it and that he would be short of staff. They worked for an independent bookstore with a minimum of employees.

The newspaper was in front of Andrea on the table, and she glanced at the headlines about the storm when her cell phone rang. She picked it up quickly and smiled when she heard Charles' voice.

Again, he began by calling her Miss Holm. She told him to call her Andrea, and they agreed on using first names. He said he had only a teenage son at home. Andrea smiled.

"I'd like to come and see you," he said. "I want to make sure you aren't going to sue me for hitting you."

Andrea's eyebrows shot up, but then she smiled. He didn't mean it because the tone of his voice said something else. She enjoyed listening to him and didn't say much. He promised to call again tomorrow.

Nana had been watching her. "This Charles fellow makes your eyes light up," she said.

"He seems to be a nice man. He might stop by one of these days," Andrea said in a casual tone of voice. She couldn't explain why she welcomed the attention of the stranger who had hit her car. She must be lonelier than she realized.

The coffee tasted good, but Andrea only nibbled on her toast. Her pain brought her back to reality. Carrying her icepack, she headed back to her bedroom.

"I'm going to the pharmacy to get your prescription," Nana said. "Then we'll see when you feel up to having company."

Andrea was anxious for Charles to call again. It would be even better to see him in person. He didn't seem to have a wife. Why was that important? Was it because she no longer had a husband? She had seen other widows forming new relationships—even after the age of 70. She was too young to live alone the rest of her life, but she certainly wouldn't settle for just any man.

Andrea's doctor recommended physical therapy and it would start in a couple of days. She watched television in the middle of the day. When nothing else was on, she ended up watching soap operas. The love scenes made her miss intimacy. She swallowed the pain pill that her mother handed her. Then she waited for Charles to call. She wondered what she would do with all her free time.

Selecting a novel that she hadn't read from her well-filled bookcase, she sat down in a corner of the sofa and began to read. Her fractured ribs made her uncomfortable, but she kept on reading.

Oh my, this is hot stuff, she thought. It almost made her forget her pain.

In the evening, Charles called and asked if he could stop by at ten o'clock in the morning. Andrea gladly said, "Yes." She looked forward to seeing him again.

Her sisters had found out about her accident and called. So did Jessica. Everyone was concerned, but Andrea was too tired to talk. After saying a few words, she gave her phone to Nana.

Andrea woke up early and stayed in bed anticipating Charles' visit. After a while, she went to the freezer, retrieved the icepack and left it on her sore spots for the required time. She felt better and decided to take a shower. To protect the wrapping around her ribcage, she used the handheld showerhead. Carefully, she washed her hair. She couldn't handle the blow dryer, but toweled her hair the best she could.

She searched her closet for something to wear. Nothing looked good with the brace. She settled for black slacks and a blue shirt. She drew a comb through her hair and applied blush to her pale cheeks. Then she had to put on that awful brace again.

When Charles pulled up in her driveway, she was full of anticipation. Standing behind the curtain, she saw him walking from his car, a bit stiffly, she thought. He held a bouquet of flowers in his hand.

He's bringing me flowers. How thoughtful.

She walked to the door and waited for the doorbell to ring. Not wanting to appear too eager, she counted to ten before opening the door. They both smiled as they greeted each other. It was the first time she saw him smile. It lit up his face and his blue eyes twinkled. He had laugh lines at the corner of his eyes.

"Perhaps these spring flowers will cheer you up," he said, handing her the bouquet.

"Thank you, Charles. I love tulips. They're beautiful." She felt like a young girl receiving flowers from a boy for the first time. Breathing in the fragrance of the tulips, she glanced at him from behind the bouquet. He wore a dark blue blazer and light slacks.

What a handsome man. He's is almost a head taller than I am.

"How come you don't have to wear a brace, Charles?"

"The airbag saved my neck. I'm sorry you're suffering, Andrea."

Andrea smiled while Charles looked her over. His eyes lowered until they had reached her feet and then quickly shot up again. She reddened and adjusted her brace. It was the first time he had seen her upright, and she hoped he liked what he saw.

"Please come in and meet my mother, Margaret Chester," she said.

Nana joined them saying, "Andrea lives alone, so I came to help her out," she said.

"That's very kind of you, Mrs. Chester."

"Let me put the tulips in water," Nana said taking them from Andrea.

"I see that you have a whiplash injury. Anything else?" Charles asked.

"I fractured a few ribs. What about you?"

"No fractured ribs, only sore muscles. I'm glad I can drive. The insurance company gave me a rental until I can buy a new car."

She motioned to Charles to follow her into the living room. Nana placed the vase with the yellow tulips on the coffee table and returned to the kitchen.

"The flowers are lovely," Andrea said. She was conscious of her brace. It didn't show her at her best.

But he's the one who hit me, so why shouldn't he see it?

He asked if her car could be fixed.

"I don't know yet. I don't even know which repair shop has my car. I have to wait until they call me."

"If you call your insurance company, they'll tell you," Charles said. "And you should ask for a rental car."

"I will. Thanks for the tip."

Andrea's eyes settled on his mouth and the cleft in his chin. He had something irresistible about him. She almost lost her concentration. She stammered as she told him she was on sick leave from her work at the bookstore, and then asked where he worked.

"At a law office."

A law office. Could he be an attorney?

She didn't want to ask, so she said, "You must be familiar with settlements?"

"Yes, although I handle mostly real-estate. We'll see if the young man who hit me from behind has insurance. He drove an older model pickup truck and looked like a college kid. As far as I'm concerned the accident was his fault."

"He might have skidded because of the rain. Perhaps he couldn't help it."

"My partner is working on it." Charles was all business at that moment.

Andrea saw a wedding band on his left hand and assumed he was a widower. She still wore her rings and was not surprised.

Nana returned from the kitchen where she had made coffee. Andrea smelled the aroma and appreciated her offer to serve them. Charles thanked her but said he had to get back to the office.

"It was good to see you, Andrea," he said as he stood up and bowed to both of them. Again, Andrea noticed how tall and sturdy he looked.

She stood behind the curtain in the living room and looked as he backed his car out of her driveway. She felt torn. As much as she liked him, she questioned his motives for visiting her. Nana startled her as she came up behind her.

"You really like this man, don't you?" she said.

"He's a pleasant gentleman, but don't read anything into it. He's an attorney. He's only concerned about my injuries because he might be made liable."

"He also wears a wedding band."

"So do I." Andrea held up her hand to show her rings. "He lives with his son."

Nana looked with surprise at her daughter, who had not taken an interest in any man since Philip died, although she had gone out to dinner a couple of times with the bookstore manager.

"I'll call my insurer and insist on a rental car. I hope I can drive with this brace on."

"Don't rush it. I can stay a few days," Nana said.

The receptionist at the insurance company put her on hold. Several minutes went by before her agent came on the phone. He said her car was at the Naperville Body Shop. She had to come there and approve the repairs.

"I need a rental car?" she said.

"Yes, it can be arranged," the agent said. "You can go to the Avis Rental Car and get one any time you feel comfortable driving."

"I also suffered an injury."

"Yes, we know. It was in the police report. Save all your statements."

It struck Andrea that Charles had not said that she could collect for her injury, suffering, and possible loss of wages. No doubt, he looked out for himself, and she would have to be careful not to put too much trust in him. She had overestimated her strength. Feeling exhausted, she went back to bed.

Nana drove Andrea to the auto shop, where the manager in charge of the repairs placed a paper in front of her to sign. She felt foolish, but she had to ask some questions.

"I'm not signing a settlement, am I?" Oh, how she wished Philip had been there with her. He always took care of the cars.

"No, you're just approving the work. There'll be a warranty on the repairs."

"The accident wasn't my fault, you know. I was hit from behind."

"We're going on what's in the report."

Andrea shuddered at the thought of Charles thinking she was out to get him, but she signed the work order. It would take a couple of weeks before she would get the car back.

When they were on their way home again, Nana echoed Andrea's thoughts.

"As an attorney, Charles will probably fight this case," she said.

"Yes, I know, and he's partial."

How could she trust him? She hated all the legalities and just wanted to get well.

Chapter 4

Two weeks had gone by. Andrea had been to physical therapy several times and could now turn her head with ease. She had the use of a rental car. Her mother had left, and Andrea felt lonely. Bob had stopped by and said he missed her both personally and as a colleague. Andrea liked him, but the owner of the bookstore frowned on dating among the employees. She had gone out twice with Bob in the past, and he had asked her when they could go out again. It wasn't easy to fit it in. One of them usually worked.

Bob was tall and slender with black, thinning hair and wore gold-rimmed glasses. Andrea had to admit that he was quite handsome. He was divorced and unattached. Yet, he paled in comparison with Charles.

Jessica had visited her several times. Her two sisters had driven all the way from Chicago's north shore to visit. Neighbors and friends had stopped in to see her. Nana called every day. Charles called occasionally. It was always good to hear his voice, but she thought it might be best not to encourage him to visit her. She watched television and read, but was tired of it all. She missed her work at the bookstore and was anxious to get back to her old routine.

Andrea sat on the examination table at her doctor's office. The doctor said the discoloration was fading, but that the soreness would last for a while longer. They took new x-rays. She should continue to wear her brace. When she asked if she could go back to work, he said, "Not yet. Come back in two weeks, and we'll see."

Two weeks! She was disappointed. It would be so boring.

The body shop called and said her car was ready. She asked Bob if he would come with her and check the work before she signed any papers, and he said he would. She hurried—as much as she was capable of hurrying—to shower and dress, and blow-dry her hair. "I have to get a haircut," she said to herself.

Forty minutes later, Bob drove up in her driveway, and she walked outside to meet him. He wore a casual jacket.

"I've been worried about you," he said with concern showing in his brown eyes.

Andrea appreciated his help, but didn't want to make it too personal since he was her boss.

"We'll take the rental car," she said matter-of-factly. "Someone from Avis will meet me at the body shop and retrieve it."

Bob folded his long legs as he sat down in the passenger seat. Andrea turned the radio on, and they listened to a morning talk show.

At the body shop, Bob walked around her car and in-spected the new paint. He bent over and looked under-neath the chassis. He crunched down without letting his knees touch the ground.

Gosh, he has a nice posterior and he's in good shape.

Bob opened and closed the trunk and all the doors. It was much more than she would have done. She would have looked at the paint job.

"It looks good on the outside," he said, "but we need to take it for a test drive to check for rattling and other problems. Do you want to come along?" She declined and gave him the keys.

"I'll be right back," he said as he put the key in the ig-nition. While Bob test-drove her car, two Avis employees arrived, and after some paperwork, one of them drove away with her rental.

Bob returned with her Ford and gave the keys to her, saying, "I believe it drives like it should, but you can take it for a spin and see what you think. You know your car."

"I believe you," she said and went into the shop to sign the papers. When she came outside, she took the driver's seat. It felt good to drive her car again. Parking it in her driveway, she asked Bob if he wanted to come in for a cup of coffee. It felt like something she had to do.

"If it isn't too much trouble?"

"It's the least I can do."

"I love to have an excuse to see you in private."

"Well, I appreciated your opinion. I hardly know any-thing about cars, other than to drive them."

His eyes flicked to hers. "How about that coffee?" he said.

"Yes, follow me."

They sat opposite each other at the kitchen table with their coffee mugs between them and talked about how it felt to live alone.

"I miss Philip so much," Andrea said. "I missed him when he traveled, but now it's all so final. He isn't coming back."

"I understand," Bob said, touching her free hand.

"He and I used to share everything. Now, when I learn something new, my first thought is to tell Philip before I realize he isn't here. I still talk to him, but I feel so alone," Andrea said, blinking away a tear.

"I react the same way," Bob said.

Andrea didn't realize that divorced people might miss their spouses in a similar way.

There was a moment of silence before Bob said, "I'd love to take you out to dinner. We could go to a movie too."

She was tired of being home all the time and had only a vague excuse. "But I'd have to wear my brace," she said.

"It won't bother me. Are you free on Saturday night?"

"Yes, Saturday would be fine. My calendar is wide open," she said with a wry smile. Going out with Bob would be better than being home alone.

Time melted away as they talked about their children. Usually, they talked about books. Bob had two young sons, but they lived with their mother. He lived in a two-bedroom apartment. "My wife got the house and the kids," he said. "I miss my boys. I see them every other weekend, but it isn't the same as having them every day. I never seem to get used to being single," he admitted.

He had lost a lot due to the divorce, Andrea thought. He had lost his wife and his children.

"I'm sorry," she said.

He looked at his watch and said, "As much as I enjoyed our chat, I need to get back to the store."

"Thanks for checking and test-driving my car."

"No problem. Thanks for the coffee."

Well, if she was going to a restaurant with Bob, she wanted to get a haircut first. She called and got an appointment the same afternoon.

When most of her hair lay on the floor, she felt so much better. The hairdresser exclaimed, "You look ten years younger." Andrea thought she looked like a boy, but the short hair would definitely be more comfortable. At least it wasn't in the way of the brace.

Driving home, she thought about Charles and compared him to Bob. Both were pleasant, but Charles had that special hold on her that she couldn't deny. She would love to see him again, but not until she could take off that awful neck brace. If Charles ever asked her out, she would accept.

She talked to Nana over the phone and told her she was going out to dinner with Bob.

"If it works out between you two, go for it. I waited too long," Nana said. "I lost my chance. The years go by so quickly, honey. Don't squander them. It's been two years since Philip died. You should look forward and not back."

Andrea wondered about the chances her mother might have had, but said nothing.

"You could invite him to dinner. He would appreciate a home-cooked meal, I'm sure."

Maybe I could do that much.

I'm surprised that Bob is still available. He's a good catch, you know,"

"Let's not go there, Nana. I want more than a good catch," Andrea snapped.

She thought of Philip.

Why did he have to die? If he hadn't become ill, we could have had a good life together for many more years.

Life is not fair.

Chapter 5

On Saturday evening, Andrea tried on three different outfits before she decided to wear a blouse and skirt. Nothing looked good with her neck brace. At least she could show off her legs. Should she continue to wear her rings that signaled she was married? If she was truly ready to move on, she should be able to remove them. She tried them on her right hand, but put them back on her left. How could she let go of Philip?

"You look lovely, Andrea," Bob said as he came to pick her up. He looked at her short hair, but did not comment.

"I feel so uncomfortable wearing this brace," she said, touching it. Deep inside, she knew it wasn't the only reason she felt uncomfortable. She was taking advantage of Bob's admiration for her.

"The brace will soon come off. You still look great to me," Bob said. She appreciated his compliment.

At the restaurant, he put her at ease by talking about the blunders he had made trying to cook decent meals for himself and his sons when they visited.

"If we go out to eat, it's usually at fast-food places," he said.

"So what was it that you were trying to cook?" Andrea asked. She was curious.

"The boys wanted mashed potatoes, but they got quite lumpy." Andrea laughed at the thought.

"It's not the easiest thing to make," she said. "You could have made it from potato flakes in a bag. I think they're called 'Instant mashed potatoes. It's not as good as homemade, but it won't get lumpy."

"I'll remember that."

Looking at the menu, he said, "It feels good to sit down at a decent restaurant in pleasant company. I think I'll have something complicated that I cannot cook, no matter how hard I try."

"And what would that be?"

"Pot roast with gravy."

"And mashed potatoes."

"Of course." He smiled broadly showing his even teeth. She returned his smile.

"It sounds terrific. I'll have the same."

While they waited for the food, Andrea asked if any new books had come in at the store.

"Yes, but let's not talk shop today," Bob said.

They enjoyed their meal. When they were finished, he put his napkin away and asked, "What movie would you like to see, Andrea?"

"I'd like to see the comedy *'Cheaper by the Dozen'* if you don't mind. It's a sequel to the movie by the same title that I saw a couple of years ago. I enjoyed it and this one is supposed to be just as funny."

"It's fine with me. I like comedies."

As they left the restaurant, Andrea startled as she saw Charles at one of the tables. He was with a woman. Andrea wished she had been that woman, but brushed the thought away and squared her shoulders. After all, she was out with another man. When she glanced back, she saw Charles looking at her legs as she walked out.

Yes! It felt good.

She and Bob laughed out loud several times during the movie. At one point, Bob put his arm around her shoulders. Both were in a good mood when they exited the theater. They linked arms and walked out like a couple. It was pleasant.

"Steve Martin didn't disappoint. He's always funny," Bob said.

"And Bonnie Hunt was good too, but 12 children!"

"It would be way too expensive for one thing. It's enough to support two," Bob said.

"Not to mention all the worries. You never stop worrying about them," Andrea said.

"As they said goodnight, he thanked her for a lovely evening and kissed her hair. At least she thought he did. Then he waited until she had unlocked the door.

"You're such a gentleman, Bob," she said.

"When can I see you again?" he asked. She had to think fast because it was so unexpected. The first thing that came to mind was Nana's advice that she should invite Bob for a home-cooked meal. She could invite their colleague, Trudy, as well.

"Would you like to come to my house for dinner some time? I'll invite Trudy too." Bob looked delighted and was quick to accept.

"Is next Sunday all right? I know you've your boys on Saturday."

"It's fine with me, but you'll have to ask Trudy."

"Shall we say six o'clock?"

"Fine, I'll bring a bottle of wine."

Why had she invited Bob? Probably because she couldn't count on Charles calling on her again.

Trudy couldn't come, so Andrea invited Nana instead. Bob looked surprised, but quickly turned to her and said, "So glad you could come, Mrs. Chester." Andrea was sure he didn't mean it. Bob had brought a bottle of red wine, and she gave him the opener before she realized that the bottle had no cork. He unscrewed the cap and asked if she wanted a glass before the meal.

"No thanks. I'd rather wait and have it with my meal," she said.

He placed the bottle on the table in the dining room where Nana was setting out the plates. The two of them chatted until Andrea suggested they go in the living room and wait until the food was ready. Nana said she would stay in the kitchen and watch the boiling pots. As Bob and Andrea entered the living room, Bob lifted Andrea's wedding picture from the piano and looked at it.

"I just wanted to see what you looked like when you were 20 or so," he said.

"I was 22."

"You were beautiful, and you still are, Andrea. Do you play the piano?"

"Not really, we bought the piano for my daughter. Here's a picture of Jessica."

"She's beautiful too, but in another way."

Sitting down, they talked about Jessica's teaching job and her boyfriend.

"I wish they would get married. They're living together," Andrea said.

"It's so common these days. At least they don't have to go through a divorce if they split." Bob sounded bitter.

This time they made conversation by talking about their common interest in books and the new titles that would be on the shelves in the near future.

"The customers are asking for you at the store," he said. "They miss you—and I miss you," he added.

"Well, that's good to hear," she said, but she was getting a little bored. She excused herself to check on the food. Bob followed her to the kitchen.

"The potatoes are ready and the carrots are almost done," Nana said. "I'll finish setting the table."

"It smells so good in here," Bob said. "You must be cooking something delicious."

"It's pot roast. You can help me lift the pot out of the oven."

She gave him the potholders and opened the oven door for him. He lifted the heavy roasting pan up on the counter, and she removed the lid and transferred the meat to a platter.

"It smells heavenly," he said. He watched her whipping the potatoes with the electric beater.

"So that's how you do it," he said.

"That's the way I do it, but you can do it with a hand beater or two forks."

"And how do you make gravy?"

"See all this juice in the roasting pan? I'll take some flour and stir it in, like this, until it bubbles. Then I add a little liquid at the time and stir again. Water from cooked vegetables is even better. Go ahead and stir, Bob." She picked up the pot with the carrots and poured the cooking water into the gravy while Bob stirred.

"The gravy needs to boil for a couple of minutes until it has the right thickness. It's already tasty. A little red wine is good though, if you would get the bottle, please."

Bob went and got the wine bottle and asked, "How much?"

"Just a little bit."

She stirred the gravy again and asked, "Do you want to taste it?"

Of course he did. She gave him a tasting spoon and took one herself. They agreed the gravy was just right.

Nana entered the kitchen and watched Bob with interests. Andrea filled their plates, and Nana helped her carry them to the dining room. Bob pulled out the chairs for the women.

"I appreciate a home-cooked meal," he said.

He filled their wine glasses and lifted his. "Here's to you, Andrea, and your speedy recovery."

"My thoughts as well," Nana said.

Bob tasted the meat first and declared it delicious. "It's better than what we had at the restaurant. I'm not surprised. It's only when I cook that restaurant food is better."

"Thank you for the compliment, Bob, but don't be so hard on yourself."

He continued to heap praise on Andrea's cooking. Every compliment came with a toast. Bob refilled their glasses although they wished he hadn't. Andrea wondered if he was nervous.

"We'll have peach pie for dessert," she said, "but I bought it at the bakery."

"Peach pie, we'll definitely drink to that."

"If you continue like this, we'll be drunk." She looked at the wine bottle and saw that it was empty. Bob's glass was also empty while hers and Nana's were still half-full.

Andrea suggested coffee in the living room. She turned on some music so it wouldn't be too quiet if the conversation stalled. Bob sat down in the larger of the two chairs, which had been Philip's favorite. Nana brought the coffee and sat down beside Andrea on the couch.

"This is the best Sunday night I've had in a long time," Bob said, glancing at Andrea.

"You're tired, aren't you?" he added.

"Yes, I am." She confessed. "I haven't regained my strength."

As soon as they had finished their coffee, Bob rose from his chair and thanked both women for a lovely evening.

Nana cleaned up in the kitchen and started the dishwasher. Andrea was fast asleep on the couch.

After her nap, Andrea asked Nana what she thought of Bob.

"He seems like a kind man. He noticed how tired you were. He's definitely interested in you. I could see it in his eyes."

"But he's my boss."

"I think he's in love with you."

"I hope not."

"I wonder what caused his divorce."

"I've wondered the same thing," Andrea said. "He never mentioned it."

On Sunday morning, Andrea got the long awaited call from Charles. He asked her if she had seen the Millennium Park.

"No, I haven't. I hear it's fantastic. I'd like to see it." She sounded almost giddy.

"Alright then, if it's not too sudden, may I pick you up at two o'clock?"

"No, it's not too soon, and yes, I'll be ready." Her heart pounded.

Chapter 6

It was a beautiful spring day, but a bit chilly. Andrea was full of anticipation. The way Charles sought her eyes held promise.

"You had a haircut?"

"Yes, do you think I look like a boy?"

"You're still very feminine, Andrea." He let his eyes slide over her body. On their way to the city, Charles said he had seen her at a restaurant a week ago.

"I saw you, too," she confessed, sounding a little shy as she cast a glance at him.

"I was there with my sister-in-law. It was her birthday," he said.

"Oh, I was there with a colleague of mine," she said in a casual voice. Charles did not comment. It was good to have that cleared up. Now they could enjoy their day together.

Charles adjusted the car temperature to her liking. She told him she had gotten her car back and that it was okay, but nothing like the Cadillac that Charles drove. Why did she say that? She wasn't jealous. She knew she admired him, but was it because of his status, his expensive car, and general affluence, or was it something more.

Charles parked the car and they headed for the long pedestrian bridge that connected the Daley Bicentennial Plaza with Millennium Park. From the bridge, they took in the breath-taking view of the Chicago skyline, Grant Park, and Lake Michigan. Trees and bushes sprouted new leaves and the daffodils and tulips were in bloom. Andrea drew in the wonderful fragrance of spring. The sun was warm, but a cold wind blew from the lake. Charles wore a windbreaker and Andrea wore a light jacket and wished she had dressed in something warmer.

"The stainless panels on the bridge create an acoustic barrier from the traffic below," Charles said. He seemed to know everything about the park. She asked him if he worked downtown.

"No, my practice is in Wheaton, but I go to the city on business once in a while."

Andrea shivered from the cold wind and hugged herself. Charles saw it and asked if she wanted his jacket. When she declined, he put both arms around her to protect her from the wind. She leaned into his warm chest and the closeness to him made her body tingle. It was wonderful to feel his arms around her. As they began to walk, Charles kept one arm around her back.

They came to the Crown Fountain with its 50-foot glass-block towers at each end of a reflecting pool. The faces projected on a large screen were flooded with water.

"Who do the faces belong to?" Andrea asked.

"I heard that they were taken from a random selection of one-thousand Chicago residents," Charles said.

"It's fantastic."

"You haven't seen the most remarkable feature of the park yet."

"There's more?"

"We're going there next."

As they approached, they could see the tourists pointing and laughing at something above them.

"What is that?" Andrea asked.

"It's the one-hundred-ton elliptical sculpture that the people of Chicago have nicknamed 'The Bean' because of its shape."

"I heard of it," Andrea said, but when they were below it, she gasped at their distorted reflections on the shiny, arched ceiling.

"Are those mirrors?" she asked.

"No, it's made of highly polished stainless steel."

They laughed at their funny shapes above, and they weren't the only ones laughing.

"This is so much fun," Andrea said. "It's a wonderful park in the center of the city."

"You haven't seen half of it yet. The Lurie Garden covers five acres and it depicts the transformation of Chicago from its marshy origins to what it is today." Charles held her elbow and adjusted his steps to hers.

"Here we are," he said. "The 15-foot-high hedge is a physical representation of Carl Sandburg's famous description of the 'City of Big Shoulders.' It also protects the perennial garden."

"I like Sandburg's poems, and I love this," Andrea said.

She enjoyed the sunshine and the spring flowers, but most of all, she enjoyed being with Charles. They walked across the footbridge that divided the garden between light and dark places.

"We'll go to the pavilion next," Charles said. "It has open-air seating for 4,000 people, and thousands more can hear the concerts just as clearly from the Great Lawn. The pavilion is the home of the Grant Park Musical Festival and many other concerts."

Charles pointed to the curved ribbons of stainless steel that arched the pavilion. A band played on stage, and they sat down and listened for a while.

"The sound is fantastic," Andrea said. She leaned her head against Charles' shoulder and closed her eyes. It was too good to be true. She felt his arm around her and inched closer to him.

"Oh, Charles, this is so wonderful. Thanks for bringing me here."

"I'm enjoying it too. Are you hungry yet?"

"No, but I'm thirsty."

"There's coffee, soda pop, and ice cream in the kiosks, and hotdogs and hamburgers by the skating arena."

"I'd like a cup of coffee to warm me up," she said.

Before Charles sat down, he took his jacket off and placed it over Andrea's shoulders. She gave him an appreciative look. The coffee and the jacket warmed her. When they had finished their coffee, she gave the jacket back to Charles, and said she would use the washroom.

"I think we've seen everything," Charles said when they were together again. "Do you want to have dinner in the city or on the way home?"

"On our way home," Andrea said. She didn't want the day to end.

"I know of a place in Wheaton close to my practice."

"Sounds good," Andrea said a little sleepily.

"I don't want to tire you out."

"No, you're not. I'm enjoying this."

More than you'll ever know.

"I could drive along the Lake Shore if you'd like to do a little sightseeing?"

"Let's do that some other time, Charles." She already hoped to see him again.

Andrea nodded off during the 45-minute car ride to Wheaton. She dreamt about the faces flooded with water and one of the faces belonged to Charles. When he turned off the ignition, she startled and woke up.

"I loved to see you sleep," he said.

"I'm sorry. I've gotten used to taking naps in the afternoon. That's why I got sleepy."

"We've done a lot of walking today."

"It was wonderful." She tried to recapture his image in her dream before it faded away, but it felt even better to look at him without the curtain of water.

"Here's the restaurant," Charles said. "I'll reserve a table, and while we wait I can show you my office, and you can rest."

She waited in the car while he made the reservation. She looked at the one-story building next to the restaurant with the sign that said, "Law Offices of Bordeaux and Brown." When Charles returned, they walked to his office, where he unlocked the door and waited for her to enter. Smiling broadly while looking at her, he said, "Here we are, pretty-face. Please come into my office."

"I don't feel pretty with this brace on," she said.

"But you are, especially when you're blushing." He was flirting with her and she was flattered.

The room had a large desk and leather furniture. A couch stood by one wall and archival cabinets along another. Charles invited her to sit on the couch, and he sat down beside her.

"Do you care for a glass of water?"

"Yes, please, water would be good." She was thirsty. He brought out bottled water from the refrigerator and poured it in two glasses. Her eyes focused on his hands and his wedding band.

"Sorry, but that's all I have here." He looked at her with his irresistible blue eyes as they quenched their thirst. She felt like she was drowning and spilled some water on the couch.

"How clumsy of me," she stammered.

"It's only water," he said wiping it up with a paper towel.

She needed a diversion. Pointing to a picture on a shelf, she asked, "Is that your son?"

48

"Yes, that's Todd. He'll graduate from high school at the end of May and has been accepted at the University of Illinois in Champaign Urbana." Charles rose and picked up another framed picture. "Here're two of my grandchildren."

"Oh, they are so cute, Charles. What are their names?"

"Danny and Ellen, they were 4 and 2 when this picture was taken. Now, they're 6 and 4. The family lives in De-Kalb. They're coming to my place for Memorial Day." He put the picture back, looked at his watch and said that their table should be ready.

As they approached the entrance to the restaurant, Charles opened the door for two women, who were coming up close behind them.

"Oh, Charles, how nice to see you," one of the women said. "I see you're not alone."

"This is Andrea Holm. Andrea, please meet Barb. I'm afraid I don't know your friend."

"Oh, I'm sorry, this is Robin," Barb said. Andrea said hello.

"What happened to your neck, Andrea?" Barb asked.

"I was in an accident." Andrea could not help noticing that Barb flirted with Charles and that Robin ogled him.

"If you would excuse us ladies, Andrea and I will go to our table," Charles said.

"Mr. Bordeaux, this way," the hostess said.

Andrea hoped that Barb and Robin would not be seated at a table close to them, but they were.

"Barb is an acquaintance. Her late husband and I used to play golf together," Charles said, referring to their encounter. In a way, Andrea felt reassured, but she also realized there were other widows who would love to date Charles. She could see Barb and Robin putting their heads together. They whispered and turned their heads to look at Charles. Barb was quite a sight with big breasts and a revealing belted knit shirt.

"You look absentminded, Andrea. May I interest you in the menu?" Charles said. He placed his reading glasses low on his nose. Andrea looked up and faced him.

"I'm sorry. You may order for me. You know the food here. I don't eat much." Barb and Robin had ruined her appetite. The waiter came and greeted Charles with a friendly, "Good evening, Mr. Bordeaux. It's unusual to see you on a weekend."

"Yes, I suppose. What do you recommend today?"

"The sirloin and the tenderloin medallions. Both are excellent."

"Would the tenderloin medallions be about right for you, Andrea?" Charles asked.

"Yes, please." She straightened in her chair. Today, she was the one who had a date with Charles.

"Then I'll have the sirloin, medium rare, and the lady will have the tenderloin."

"How do you want your tenderloin done, ma'am?"

"Medium rare, please."

"We've the same preference," Charles said. Andrea loved getting to know Charles' preferences.

When they left the restaurant, Barb and Robin were right behind them.

"How's your family, Charles?" Barb asked.

"Everybody is fine."

"Will you start playing golf soon?"

"I imagine so."

"I'd love to play with you sometime."

"I've promised to play with my partner," Charles said. "Have a nice day." He bowed to the ladies.

"It was good seeing you, Charles."

"Goodbye," Andrea said curtly. Charles cupped her elbow and they headed for the car.

That woman was not going to give up. If she's that aggressive in front of me, how far will she go if she found Charles alone somewhere?

"Sorry about the interruption," Charles said.

"I'd love to play golf with you when I'm well again."

"I'd like that."

Charles drove her home and said goodbye at her door. "Thanks for a wonderful day," he said before kissing her on her forehead and giving her a hug. She hugged him back and they held each other for a moment.

"I'm afraid I've tired you out, but perhaps we can go out again sometime?" He leaned forward and peered into her eyes.

Andrea met his gaze. "Yes, I'd like that. I enjoyed our day together."

"I'll call you," he said as he turned slowly and walked to his car. She remained by the door and waved as he drove away. He waved back. Somehow, she thought he would call her again, and oh, how she hoped he would.

Chapter 7

Another beautiful spring day greeted Andrea as she picked up her morning paper from the stoop. She wished she could work in the yard. The lawn needed mowing. Old leaves from last year littered the ground and the flowerbeds. Her late tulips bloomed and reminded her of the tulips Charles had given her.

She was still thinking about Charles when she sat in the waiting room of her doctor's office leafing through magazines until her name was called.

The doctor was pleased with her progress and said she no longer had to wear her brace. Best of all, she could go back to work. That's what she had been waiting to hear.

"Hello Bob," she greeted her boss as she walked into the bookstore.

"Andrea, good to see you again. Are you coming back to work?" He sounded hopeful.

"Yes, my doctor okayed it."

"Good. You can start right away. I need you to work the next three weekends."

"That's not fair. It's supposed to be every other weekend."

"Sorry, but I worked three weekends in a row while you were sick. You didn't use to mind working weekends." He raised his eyebrows as if he had a question.

"I know, but three weekends?"

"If you're going to continue working fulltime, you still have to work weekends and evenings. I'm sorry, Andrea, but I can't make an exception for you."

"It's alright." He was the boss. Andrea walked to the back room, put away her purse, and signed in. She needed to work fulltime to get her benefits. As long as she didn't have to lift any heavy boxes of books, she would be alright.

The store was large. It sold mostly books, but also magazines, greeting cards, wrapping paper, and gift items. She took her place behind the counter and readied the cash register. Her first customer waited for her with a book in his hand. "Have a nice day," she said as the customer left with his purchase. She never said, "Have a great day," because she remembered how hard it had been to hear that when Philip was seriously ill. The day went fast, and she didn't have time to think about anything but serving her customers.

Back home, she felt stiff and tired. She ate leftovers from the fridge, soaked in the tub, and went to bed. The next day, she would begin work at ten when the store opened. On Wednesday, she had a day off.

If only I could see Charles then... but he would probably be working.

To her delight, he called on Tuesday evening, and asked when she could have lunch with him.

"Wednesday is my day off," she said in a low voice, but her heart pumped a little faster.

"So you're back at work then?"

"Yes, I am."

"All right, I'll rearrange my schedule." It was more than Andrea had expected.

Over lunch, they talked about her work hours. Charles asked if she could go out with him on Saturday night, and she agreed although she knew she would be tired after working a full day.

"I'll get off work at six," she said.

"May I pick you up at the book store then?"

"Yes, you may, Charles."

"See you Saturday night, pretty-face," he said as he left her outside her door. He bent down and kissed her on the cheek. He hugged her a little tighter than last time.

"Is 'pretty-face' going to be my nickname?"

"Until I can call you something else."

Charles left her with many happy thoughts. What did he mean by saying, "Until I can call you something else?" She wondered if she could stop feeling married to Philip. Her mother had said she should look forward and not back. So why did she feel a little guilty? Was it because of Jessica?

With the afternoon off, Andrea decided to go and visit her daughter. There were at least two messages from her on the answering machine. Jessica's classes were over for the day, and she was probably at home correcting papers.

Andrea enjoyed driving her car. She went north on Naperville Road, skirted Danada Park, and turned right on Roosevelt Road. She looked for Charles' office and as she stopped for a red light and glanced at his parking spot. His car wasn't there. He had said he would be working.

Oh, well, he could be meeting with a client. He could be at his insurance agent's office. He could be looking for a new car for himself. He could be playing golf with Barb. It's none of my business. Not yet, anyhow.

She parked the car outside Jessica's apartment building and called her daughter's number.

"Honey, it's me."

"Mom, why aren't you ever home when I call you?"

"I've been busy."

"Busy? You're supposed to be recuperating."

"I'm not going to tell you over the phone. I'm outside your building. Buzz me in. I'm back to work."

"Come on up, Mom."

"There's something I want to tell you," Andrea said after a quick hug and kiss.

"Let's sit down in the kitchen then, and I'll make some tea." Jessica poured water in the teakettle and placed on the burner.

"Let's hear it."

"My social life has definitely improved. First, I went out to dinner with Bob. Then Charles invited me to go to the Millennium Park." Andrea felt weird telling her daughter she had two gentlemen callers.

"Who's Charles?" Jessica's voice rose. "You were just in an accident."

"It has to do with my accident. Charles is the one who hit my car."

Jessica opened her eyes wide. "Now, that's a story if I ever heard one. Didn't you get angry with him when he hit you?"

"No, not really, he couldn't help it. He's so pleasant and caring. He has shown his concern for me more than once."

The teakettle whistled and Jessica turned off the gas flame. She didn't say anything until the tea steeped in the pot.

"Are you sure you're no longer in mourning, Mom?"

"I'll always love and miss your dad, but it's been two years, Jessica."

"What about Bob? He seems like an honest, upright fellow."

"Yes, I know, and he always looks at me with longing puppy eyes. With Charles, it's different. I don't know much about him other than he's a lawyer."

"So you've two men interested in you. Not bad, Mom!" Andrea didn't think there was any admiration in her daughter's voice.

"Don't make too much of it, Jessica."

"You might be married for the second time before I'm married at all." Now, Andrea could hear a little bitterness in Jessica's voice.

"Isn't that up to you? Or does it depend on Jason?"

"We've agreed to wait." Jessica looked uncomfortable.

"Now, tell me about Charles. Does he have a family?"

Andrea eagerly told her daughter everything she knew about Charles's family and rushed into her errand.

"I'd like to go out and buy a new outfit to wear next Saturday when Charles takes me to dinner. Would you go with me to a store?"

"I suppose I could. A boutique here has a sale right now. But we'd have more to choose from if we went to a mall."

"Let's go and see what they have in that little boutique. I don't have to buy anything today, but it would be fun to look."

"I'd like to meet Charles," Jessica said as they approached the store. Jessica acted more like a concerned mother than daughter, Andrea thought.

The service in the boutique was far superior to any service in the big shopping centers. The salesclerk said she had several dresses she thought would look good on Andrea.

"With your figure, it shouldn't be hard to fit you. How about a black cocktail dress?" she asked.

"I don't think I need one of those. Don't you have any two-piece dresses?"

"Yes, here's a blue one that I think will fit you." Andrea liked it and went to the fitting room to try it on.

"It looks great on you, Mom," Jessica said.

"I could wear it with or without the jacket."

"It fits you perfectly," the clerk said."

"So you don't want the cocktail dress? Do you even have one, Mom?" Jessica asked.

"No, but I can always buy one later—should I ever be invited to a cocktail party."

She paid for her purchase, and felt happy, but she also felt guilty. Perhaps Jessica wanted a new dress. "May I buy you something, honey?" she asked.

"Thanks for asking, Mom, but not today."

As Andrea drove up her driveway, Ernie Anderson from next door came over and said hello.

"I saw you wearing a neck brace earlier, and now your grass needs mowing. Would you allow me to that for you?"

"I would be most grateful, Ernie. Thank you so much for offering. I was in an automobile accident and can't do it for a while."

"Don't worry about it. I'll take care of it until you can do it yourself. I need the exercise."

"Thank you so much. I'll be glad to pay you."

"No need. One day you might be able to do something for me. How's your mother?"

"She's fine. Do you ever go back to Rockville, Ernie?"

"Yes, I go there sometimes to see my friends and your mother."

Chapter 8

While making plans for her dinner date with Charles, Andrea got a call from her insurance company.

"Mrs. Holm," the agent said, "Your claim has been denied."

"Excuse me."

"The compensation for your accident and personal injury."

"Against whom?"

"Mr. Charles Bordeaux."

"I didn't make a claim against him."

"He was the one who hit you."

"I know, but the driver at fault was the one in the third car."

"Well, there could be circumstances in which.... Anyhow, I have this statement from Mr. Bordeaux saying he assumes no responsibility for the accident."

"And are you telling me he denied that he hit me?"

"Not exactly, but he refuted your claim."

"It's not my claim. It's yours." Andrea felt anger creeping up inside her. She was angry with the insurer and she was angry with Charles.

"Well, it's complicated. Perhaps you want to consult a lawyer, Mrs. Holm?"

"I might just do that," she snapped. The lawyer she had in mind was Charles Bordeaux.

She was upset and bewildered. How could Charles do this to her?

Because, he has only pretended to like me.

The thought hurt so much that she began to cry. How could she have been so foolish? Her anger surfaced again, but now she was angry at herself. She had allowed herself to be duped by Charles' charm and had to face it. He was a lawyer and he had misled her. It was obvious he looked out for his own interest.

Charles had said she could call him at his office. She would do that and demand an explanation. She dialed his number and regretted it as soon as she heard the receptionist answering, "Bordeaux and Brown."

"Mr. Bordeaux, please." She might as well go through with it before she changed her mind.

"May I ask who's calling?"

"It's Andrea Holm."

"Just a minute, please."

"Andrea. This is a nice surprise. What can I do for you?" The sound of his voice made her feel weak and uncertain about the reason for her call, but she plowed ahead.

"I can't go out with you on Saturday night. My insurance agent called...." A hiccup interrupted her answer.

"And what did he have to say?"

"He..." *hiccup*... "said..." *hiccup*... "That..." *hiccup*.... "I can't talk."

"Are you at home?"

"Yes." Another hiccup. It was hopeless. She let out a wimpy cry.

What's the matter with me? I sound like a child.

"I'm coming. I can't understand what you're trying to say. I'll see you in a little while. I just have to make some calls first. Try to calm down. It can't be that bad."

Andrea hung up and bawled. How could she compose herself before he came? She had to wash her face, but her eyes would still be red. Well, he might as well see the damage he had done. It would be worth thousands of additional dollars in compensation for extreme suffering.

She had composed herself several times before he came, but as soon as she thought about his deceit, the tears came back. Feeling like a fool, she went to open the door for him. He held a box in one hand.

"What's the matter? Have you been crying?"

"It's your fault." Then the darn hiccups started again.

"So, so, let's sit down and talk this through." He led her to the couch in the living room. Her legs felt wobbly. She sank down on the couch, and Charles sat down beside her.

"I think I know why you're upset," he said looking at her. "I talked to my partner who's handling the claim. The papers he filed were routine. It doesn't mean you won't be compensated. Your agent shouldn't have called you. He should've known better."

Andrea wiped her tears and felt calmer but still angry.

"So it's his fault?"

"I'm not trying to shift blame. I should have checked into it myself. I'm so sorry. Can you forgive me?" He tilted his head and looked irresistible.

"I thought I had to get a lawyer who was on my side." She sounded wimpy and she knew it.

"No, you don't, pretty-face. I have your interest at heart, very much so." He looked defeated.

"Well, I'm glad to hear it."

"So am I forgiven?" He leaned his head forward and to one side while looking into her eyes.

"Yes." She was a bundle of nerves and welcomed the relief that flooded through her.

"Then, here're some cookies for you. I think you need some comfort food. We had these in the office, and I didn't have time to get anything else."

"Thank you, Charles."

"Your insurance agent won't bother you again. He jumped the gun and my partner told him so."

"I don't know why I cried," she said.

"Perhaps because you're disappointed in me and you want me to be on your side?"

"Maybe." A smile spread on her face.

"So are we still on for Saturday night, pretty-face?"

"Yes, but my face is not pretty."

"I think it's very pretty. I like your sensitive side."

"You probably think I cry all the time, but I don't. I haven't cried so much since Philip died."

"I believe you. I'm flattered that you cried over me. How long ago is it that your husband died?"

"Two years."

"It's one year since my wife Elaine died."

"Oh. Do you feel lonely?"

"Yes, I do."

"Would you stay for a cup of coffee?"

"I'd be glad to. I don't want to quarrel with you," he said.

"And I don't want to quarrel with you. Let's call it a misunderstanding."

She felt like a fool, but a happy fool. They stood up and walked to the kitchen.

"Now, allow me to make the coffee," he said.

Andrea watched as Charles made himself at home in her kitchen. "One measure to the cup," he said, as he measured out the coffee into the filter. She liked him in her kitchen.

He opened doors and drawers until he found the mugs, sugar, milk, and teaspoons. They sat down at the kitchen table. Being with Charles and watching the coffee drip was heaven. He stroked her hands, picked them up, and kissed them. The coffee stopped dripping and was ready.

"Now, let's see if my coffee is as good as yours," he said. "I see that you're smiling, so you probably don't think so."

"I know it's as good as mine because I saw you measuring the coffee. Since you're so good in my kitchen, would you please heat some milk for me?"

"Hot milk coming up, ma'am. Now, where're those cookies that I brought?"

"They're still in the living room. I'll go and get them."

While they munched on the cookies and drank the coffee, Charles said, "This is the best coffee break I had in a long time."

"I feel the same way. Thank you for coming to cheer me up, Charles. I don't think I could have gone to work this afternoon if you hadn't come."

"Remember, this was a private visit. I didn't come to you as a lawyer."

"I appreciate that."

"I'm so glad I met you, even if it was by accident," he said. They both laughed. It was so much better than crying.

"I need to go now. You take care of yourself, pretty-face. No more tears."

"No more tears. I promise."

He pecked her on the cheek. Andrea felt much better. By coming to her in her hour of need, Charles had shown that he cared for her.

Before her dinner date with Charles, Andrea twirled her wedding rings on her finger once again. It was time to take them off. She was sure of it. Or was it too soon? She slid them off and looked in the jewelry box for another ring to wear when her eyes fell on Philip's ring. She picked it up and thought about their wedding day. She had been happy then, but Philip was dead, and she had to move on. She put his ring back and tried on a ring with a sapphire stone that she hadn't worn for a long time. It still fit. Would she feel foolish if Charles still wore his ring? He might not even notice that she had switched rings.

Chapter 9

Charles walked into the bookstore shortly before six. He wore a bluish-gray suit, white shirt and a blue tie that was the color of her dress. Andrea's heart skipped a beat.

"It will be a few minutes before I'm ready," she said. "I have to close the store." She was glad that Bob had gone home for the day. Charles looked at the book displays.

"What do you like to read, Charles?" she asked.

"I don't read much fiction, but I've read a couple of John Grisham's books."

"He's a lawyer like you."

At six o'clock sharp, she hung the "Closed" sign on the door and locked it.

"I'll be right back," she said before walking to the back room to take off her smock and put on her dress jacket. She kicked off her comfortable shoes and slipped into heels. A touch of lipstick and she was ready.

"You look transformed," he said as she walked toward him. "Nice dress."

"Thank you." She felt the heat in her cheeks.

When they were outdoors, she looped her arm in his and he led her to a brand new car.

"When did you get this?"

"I got it Wednesday afternoon."

Oh, that's why I didn't see his rental car in his parking spot. I knew there would be an explanation.

They talked about their children while driving to the restaurant. She already knew he had two sons. The youngest, Todd, lived at home, and his other son lived in DeKalb. Now, she learned that he also had a married daughter.

"I've only one child, my daughter, Jessica, and she said she would like to meet you," Andrea said.

"If she's anything like her mother, I'll like her." That was a nice compliment and it gave Andrea courage to ask, "Does Todd know about me?"

"I've told him. He asked if you were *hot*, and I said you are. Now, he can't wait to see you." Charles winked and smiled.

"How can I live up to those expectations?"

"You're *hot* to me, and you're beautiful." Andrea reddened and hoped that Charles didn't see it. She *felt* hot all over.

He parked the car, took her hand and squeezed it.

"Perhaps we could plan on you coming to my barbecue on Memorial Day and meet the clan?"

"I'd love to meet your family, but it will make me nervous."

"You've nothing to worry about."

As they walked from the parking lot they admired the blooming tulips that seemed to be everywhere in the downtown area.

Charles asked Andrea to pose for a picture in front of a flowerbed filled with red tulips along the River Walk.

"You go so well together with the tulips," he said.

They listened to the glockenspiel from the Moser Tower that commemorated the end of the Civil War.

"Have you been up in the tower, Charles?" Andrea asked.

"No, I haven't. I suppose you have."

"Yes, I've climbed the 253 steps to the top, but I was younger then. The tower is 160 feet high and houses a museum."

They entered the restaurant and Charles led her to their table and pulled out the chair for her. He no longer wore his wedding band.

He has taken it off, just like I have taken off mine.

It made her heart sing.

Charles had his glasses in his breast pocket, but didn't use them to read the menu. Instead, he asked the waiter what he recommended. Andrea chose the salmon and Charles did, too.

"I don't like to prepare fish at home," Andrea said, "so sometimes I like to have it when I eat out."

"I feel the same way," Charles said. Again, they agreed. The evening was going well.

While they waited for their food, Charles asked, "What are you doing for Mother's Day?"

"Since I can't go and see my mother, she's coming to me. Jessica's coming too, but not until after I've closed the store. Then we'll go out to eat, the three of us."

"My mother is 85-years old. I'll take her out to an early dinner. Then I guess Todd and I will go to the cemetery."

"I'll do that sometime before Memorial Day," Andrea said. It was something else they had in common. "I also need to plant some flowers at home."

"I don't know how to plant flowers."

"I could show you."

It would be another reason for us to be together.

"I'd like that."

Their conversation flowed easily while they enjoyed the meal and a glass of white wine.

"Do you have any brothers and sisters, Andrea?" he asked. They wanted to know each other better, and that included family members. Nothing wrong with that, Andrea thought.

"Two sisters and they both live on the north shore."

"My brother lives in Colorado. I've no siblings here."

"You mentioned Memorial Day before. I'm free then." She didn't want him to forget his tentative invitation.

"Then you can come to my house for the barbecue?"

"I'd be glad to come." It seemed like she always agreed with Charles, but why wouldn't she when she liked him so much?

When they were in his car, Andrea asked, "Could you please take me to the bookstore so I can get my car?" She regretted she hadn't told him to pick her up at home. Their evening would be over, and she'd be driving home alone.

"Of course, but it's early. Do you want to do something else?"

"Well, I rented a movie that I'd like to see." Andrea preferred to see a movie with Charles at home rather than in a movie house.

"What's the movie?"

"*The Road to Perdition.* I understand it's about a gangster who lived in Rock Island. It's also about bank robberies in Chicago. It's supposed to be good, but I think it's also scary. It's not what I usually watch."

"I haven't seen it, so I'll accept your invitation."

While Charles followed her in his car, she thought about the last time he drove behind her—when they had the accident. As much as she had suffered, it had been worth it because she had met him.

Once they were in her living room, Andrea felt warm and took off her jacket, exposing her bare arms.

"You look marvelous. You really are hot," he said. He gave her a light hug. Her legs went almost numb. She motioned to him to sit down on the couch while she started the DVD player. When the movie began, she sat down beside him.

The guns went off repeatedly and people were shot and killed. Andrea didn't like it when the gangster killed the young boy. She moved closer to Charles and grabbed his hand. He put his arm around her, and it made her feel much better.

When the movie was over, Charles said. "It showed some human emotions among all the violence. It was touching to see how the gangster, played by Tom Hanks, protected his surviving son."

"And then he taught his son to drive the car. That part was funny."

When the movie was over, Charles reached for her.

"I'd like to hold you, and I must do it now," he said.

"I'm not stopping you." She smiled invitingly.

He kissed her neck. She sought his lips and drowned in his embrace. She wanted to rip off his tie and coat, but she didn't have to. He took them off himself. She slid her hand into his shirt opening and felt his chest hair.

"Do you know what that does to me?" he moaned. His kisses got hotter and deeper.

"I like you, Andrea," he said.

"I like you, Charles." It was too early to call it love, but the sparks flew between them.

"It's wonderful to have these feelings, isn't it?"

"It is. I feel like a teenager."

He stroked her bare arms and kissed them all the way to her fingertips.

"I see that you're wearing a different ring today," he said.

"And you're not wearing your ring."

"It means we think alike."

"I'm glad you don't have a kid who can come home and surprise us," he said in a gravelly voice.

"We're adults."

"Yes. I'm 55. I might be too old for you?"

"No, you're perfect. I'm 52."

"You look younger than 52, and you're still hot." He blew on his fingers to emphasize.

"I'm glad I can still excite a man."

"I think I better leave before you excite me even more."

He stroked her hair out of her face. They kissed again and looked longingly at each other.

"I love your eyes and lips," he said.

"I love your blue eyes and your kisses make me dizzy."

He kissed her nose and the dimples in her cheeks.

"The best is yet to come, pretty-face, but you need to get stronger."

Before what?

He made her blood rush so fast she could hear it in her ears.

With his arms around her, Charles looked into her eyes, saying, "Todd graduates next weekend and my gift to him is a trip to Europe. He's going to be hiking in Ireland with a buddy for a few weeks. I'll be all alone, and then we can have more time together, if it's alright with you?"

"Oh, yes. When is he leaving?" She hoped she didn't sound too anxious.

"He leaves after Memorial Day."

It was more than she could have hoped for in her wildest dreams.

"I can't wait to see you again," he said.

"Would you like to come for dinner next Saturday and meet my daughter and her boyfriend?" Andrea asked.

"Yes, I would, but you said you're working late."

"I can prepare the dinner in advance." She knew that nothing was impossible for her when it came to Charles.

"I'll bring the wine. May I bring something else?"

"You can bring ice cream if you want."

Charles hung his tie loose around his neck and slung his coat over one shoulder.

Oh my, he looks boyish despite his gray hair.

She stood on tiptoe as they kissed at the door. "Thanks for a wonderful night, pretty-face," he said. "The attraction between us is undeniable."

"I feel it too."

"I guess it's an accidental attraction."

"We could say that." It made her very happy that Charles was as attracted to her as she was to him.

She thought about Charles for several days and nights until she received a surprise call from Copenhagen. Philip's younger brother, Kristian, was on a business trip to Chicago and had to remain longer than anticipated. He stayed at a hotel and drove a rental car.

"I have some free time, so I wondered if I could come and see you?" he asked.

"Of course, Kristian, but I work and I can't take time off."

"That's alright. I thought I could take you out to dinner, that's all."

They decided on Thursday evening. Kristian would pick her up at seven o'clock.

After Kristian had graduated from college, he had decided to do some graduate work in Denmark. Philip and Kristian's parents were from Denmark, and the family had relatives there. Kristian studied the Danish language for a while, got a job with a global company, where he used English, extended his visa, and decided to stay. He had visited a couple of times when Jessica was a child. He had been engaged to a Danish woman, but as far as Andrea knew, they were not married.

Kristian rang her doorbell exactly at seven o'clock. Andrea gasped in disbelief when she saw him. He looked so much like Philip it was almost as if her husband had come alive. Not having seen Kristian for years, she had missed how he had matured. He was ten years younger than Phil.

"You're as attractive as ever, Andrea," he said with a big smile and an admiring glance at her. "I was always a little jealous of Philip, but now I'm so sorry he's gone. It must have been hard for you."

Andrea nodded. She didn't know what to say. It had been very difficult. Now, it felt so strange to be with someone who looked and sounded like Philip. Kristian was as tall and broad-shouldered as her husband had been and moved and gestured the same way.

"You remind me so much of Philip it's uncanny," she finally said.

"I suppose so," he said. "I've seen pictures."

When they were in the car, Kristian said that the American-owned company he worked for wanted him to move to Chicago and head up a trading division. He was thinking about it.

"Sounds terrific! How long will you be staying?"

"Until next week—I'd like to meet Jessica, too."

Andrea filled him in about Jessica. "She and her boyfriend are coming to my house for dinner on Saturday night," she said. "Would you like to come?"

"Very much so. I don't have anything scheduled for the weekend."

"It's settled then." She didn't tell him there would be one other guest. She had a delightful evening alone with Kristian. It almost felt like she was out with Philip. A couple of times, she called him Phil. There wasn't a moment of silence between them. Kristian told Andrea about his broken engagement. "Now, I don't have anyone keeping me in Denmark. I'm free to move to Chicago," he said.

Andrea couldn't deny that she was attracted to Kristian, but could it be because he reminded her so much of Phil?

It was Saturday, and Andrea had just come home from work. She had prepared most of the dinner in advance and the table was set. All she had to do was heat the chicken cacciatore, cook the noodles, make the salad, and change her clothes.

Jessica and Jason arrived first. Kristian arrived next with flowers for Andrea. Charles was in shirtsleeves when he came, but carried his jacket. He brought two bottles of French wine and a tub of well-packaged Whitey's ice cream. Andrea introduced him as a dear friend, but she could see Jessica winking her eye at Kristian. Andrea put the ice cream in the freezer and handed Charles a bottle opener. She was quite certain that Charles' wine bottles had corks.

They looked at each other and remembered the last time in her living room. Andrea felt warm all over.

When they were all seated at the table, Charles raised his glass and proposed a toast to the "charming hostess."

Kristian couldn't stop talking about old times. He reminisced about growing up with Philip, telling stories that neither Andrea nor Jessica had heard before. Andrea's eyes filled with tears. Charles looked at her, and then at Kristian, who had her full attention.

Charles and Jason were the outsiders. They talked about computers. Jason installed computer systems, and before the dinner was over, Charles had given him his business card and invited him to come to the office to show what he had to offer.

After dessert, Kristian declared that it was early morning in Denmark. "If I stay up any longer, I'll go to sleep in my chair," he said.

When the life of the party had left, Charles also said goodnight. Andrea followed him to the door. "I hope you didn't mind that my brother-in-law came," she said.

"Of course not." He kissed Andrea on the mouth before he left and said he would call. Andrea thought the dinner had gone well, but she couldn't wait to hear what Jessica had to say about Charles.

"He's a good-looking older gentleman," she said. "But Uncle Kristian is so cool, and he reminds me of Dad."

Andrea smiled. She couldn't agree more about Kristian, but she had a hard time thinking of Charles as an "older gentleman" although he probably was to Jessica. Charles had looked a little old compared to Kristian, who still had a full head of wavy, blond hair. Charles' hair, what was left of it, was straight and so gray it was almost white.

"I think that Kristian felt a need to talk about his brother," Andrea said. "In the beginning, I felt the same need to talk about your dad. Kristian's sense of loss may have intensified when he came here."

"I think you're right, Mom, but I loved learning more about Dad."

"I did, too, and now I feel guilty about not being here for Kristian on Memorial Day, but as you know, I promised Charles to come to his family gathering."

"It would be great if we could have a barbecue here, the four of us, since Jason and I don't have a yard."

"I'll think about it, but I'd feel bad about turning Charles down."

"I think he'll understand since Kristian is only here for a couple of days," Jessica said in a pleading voice.

When Jessica and Jason had left, Andrea thought about Charles. Was she good enough for him or did she fool herself in thinking so? Did he date her because he was lonely and needed a woman in his life? Those were serious questions. Was she ready to meet his family? Wasn't it too early? Perhaps it would be best to wait. Was she attracted to Kristian because he reminded her of Philip? What about if he stayed in Chicago? He was family, and no matter what, she couldn't shut him out.

Chapter 10

Kristian called Andrea to ask her if she'd go with him to the cemetery and show him Philip's grave. He'd been in Asia on business when Philip died and had missed his funeral. There was no way Andrea could refuse, and since she had planned to go to her husband's grave anyway before Memorial Day, she accepted at once. She brought flowers and so did Kristian.

Standing by Philip's grave, Andrea arranged the two bouquets together in one vase and stood back to see the full effects.

"It looks nice don't you think?" she asked Kristian.

"It does. I miss my brother so much." His voice broke.

Andrea took out a blanket from her car, spread it on the grass, and invited Kristian to sit down beside her. When he did, he buried his face in his hands.

Andrea placed a hand on his shoulder.

"I know how you feel," she said. "It's a shock to see the headstone for the first time. I've been sitting here alone crying many times," she said. "I appreciate your company."

"Will you be buried here?" he asked.

"I suppose so. I didn't want my name on the stone yet. It's hard enough to see Philips names and dates."

"Because I moved to Denmark we missed out on many years together."

"You didn't know that he would die."

"But I wish I had come home when I heard he was ill."

"I know. He probably didn't tell you how ill he was."

"No, he did not. It wasn't like him to complain. I didn't know he'd die."

"Sometimes people die suddenly in accidents, like your parents did, and we're totally unprepared."

She told Kristian about her injury in the recent three-car accident. "I thought I would die of a heart attack. Life is so fragile. All three of us could have died in the crash, like your parents did. It was Charles and another, younger man. Luckily, we maintained a low speed due to the bad weather."

"So that's how you met Charles?" She nodded.

"Thanks for bringing me here, Andrea. It helped me get closure."

It didn't surprise Andrea that Kristian wanted to go to the cemetery where his parents were buried. "I'll do it tomorrow morning," he said.

Kristian had touched her heartstrings by showing his feelings. It was obvious that he mourned his brother. Andrea felt strongly that she wanted to be with him and Jessica on Memorial Day. It was wrong to be anywhere else.

Without hesitation, she asked if he wanted to spend Memorial Day at her house with Jessica and Jason.

"I'd love to," he said.

"We could have a barbecue in my back yard. Phil usually took care of the grilling, and now I'll let you do the honor."

"Terrific. I'll be there."

They stood up and Andrea began to fold the blanket.

"I need to go and buy annuals for my flower beds," she said. "Do you want to come along?"

"I have nothing else to do."

They brought home petunias and geraniums and got ready to plant them. Kristian borrowed Phil's work clothes that still hung in a closet in the basement. Now, he looked even more like her husband. Andrea felt a tug in her heart as she looked at him.

She decided where the flowers would go, and Kristian dug the holes. When they were finished, she watered them. "Now, I'm thirsty," she said. "Let's go inside and get something cold to drink."

She took off her crocs and sprayed them with the hose. Kristian told her that crocs were also popular in Europe. Andrea walked barefoot into the house but slipped into another pair of shoes once she was inside. If Kristian had the same taste as Phil, he wanted a beer, and she had some in her refrigerator. She had read his mind, he said. She placed two bottles of beer on the table and brought out bread, ham, and cheese. After they had eaten, Kristian said he needed a shower before changing clothes.

"You can shower in the basement if you like. That's what Phil always did."

She listened to the shower go on in the basement and imagined that Phil was there. She could almost see Phil in Kristian's body. They were like twins. It disturbed her, but it was also comforting, she thought as she headed for her own shower.

She was almost done when she heard Kristian call her name.

"I'm in the bathroom," she said, peeking out through the door.

"Oh, sorry."

Just as she closed the door, her towel dropped to the floor. It was embarrassing although he couldn't have seen much through the crack in the door. She dressed quickly. She'd forgotten to call Charles.

When she came into the living room, Kristian had turned on the television and watched golf.

"I like golf," he said, "but I prefer football. We don't have American football in Denmark."

"If you'd excuse me, Kristian, I've a couple of telephone calls to make."

"Go ahead," he said. "I'm not going anywhere."

She went to the kitchen to telephone Charles.

"Charles, I'm so sorry, but I can't come to your barbecue tomorrow. Kristian is here for only a couple of days. He's family, and Jessica and I feel we should entertain him with a barbecue at my place. He's mourning his brother and needs to be with family."

"I understand. You don't have to apologize."

"I'll be glad to come some other time," she said. They talked some more, but she could hear the disappointment in his voice. She would have to make it up to him. Then she called Jessica, and no problem there. She and Jason would come. When Andrea walked into the living room, the golf game had gone to commercial.

"Everything is set for tomorrow," she said." I just need to buy the food."

"How about we go out to eat and then buy the food on the way home?" he suggested.

"We could do that."

"Great, do you want to watch the rest of the game with me?" He patted the couch beside him, but she sat down in a chair. She had watched many sports with Philip, so why not?

She thought of Philip and how he, too, had preferred football. He was always fully engaged in the game. He yelled at the players and the coach like they could hear him. He gestured with his arms and reached toward the television screen. He cheered loudly, and with each touchdown, he stood up and either cheered or moaned depending on which team made the touchdown.

"I played football in high school, just like Phil," Kristian said. I always admired my big brother. Whatever he did, I wanted to do."

Andrea felt attracted to Kristian, but was it because he reminded her of Phil? Or was it because they had so much in common?

Finally, the game was over and Kristian turned to Andrea and said, "Let's go. I'm hungry."

Seated opposite each other at the restaurant, Andrea asked Kristian if he had come to a decision about the job offer in Chicago.

"I'm interested, but I need to find out about the salary, commissions and benefits. Vacations aren't as long here as in Denmark. I'll insist on the same vacation time that I have now. I'll know more on Tuesday after I meet with the board. I enjoy being here. I feel so much at home with you and Jessica and Jason." Phil's name remained unspoken, but it hung in the air.

At the grocery store, Kristian offered to buy the food. "The meat is cheaper here," he said, as he picked out the most expensive cuts. Andrea selected baking potatoes, fresh asparagus, and a few tarts for dessert.

As they unloaded the groceries and put them away, Kristian said, "It's late, so I think I'll say goodnight. Thanks for today, sweet Andrea. I'm looking forward to tomorrow." He pecked her on the cheek and was off. He was like a breath of fresh air blown in from Europe. He was a hot, live wire that she was afraid to touch.

Kristian had made her think more about Phil than she had since she met Charles. Watching television with Kristian had meant revisiting Sunday afternoon sports with Phil. She could get excited about sports, but not as much as the men could. She wondered if Charles was a football fan. Weren't all American men?

On Memorial Day, Kristian learned that Jason was a huge Chicago Bears fan.

"If you come back in the fall, I could get tickets," Jason said.

"When I return, it will be either on a business trip or to live here, and then I'll take you up on your offer, Jason."

Kristian put the steaks on the grill, and Jason watched. He wanted his rare, and he was the only one.

Andrea and Jessica were in the kitchen getting the potatoes out of the oven and steaming the asparagus.

"I'm so glad we could have this afternoon together with Uncle Kristian, and I hope he'll come back to live here. He's super attractive. He'd have a ton of women chasing him," Jessica said.

Andrea had to agree with Jessica's assessment. Kristian wouldn't be available for long and neither would Charles, she thought.

The weather was perfect, but later in the evening a rain shower chased them indoors. Their congenial talk continued in the living room over coffee and tarts.

"Uncle Kristian," Jessica said. "I want you to come back here, but if you stay in Denmark, I'd like to come and visit. I'd love to see Copenhagen."

"I'd be glad to show you all the sights, but don't call me uncle. You're a grown woman now, Jessica. You can call me Kris."

Jason began to call him Kris, but Jessica and Andrea continued to call him Kristian.

When her guests had left, Andrea called Charles.

How did your party go?" she asked.

"Fine, except for my sister-in-law. She's the trouble-maker, but I don't want to talk about her. When can I see you?" Apparently, he was ready to continue where they had left off. But was she? Of course, she had to see Charles again and find out if the magic was still there.

"I'm free on Wednesday," she said. Charles accepted. "I'll take the afternoon off. I'll come over after lunch and we can decide what to do."

Chapter 11

Kristian called and said he was returning to Copenhagen, but would relocate to Chicago as soon as possible. He had accepted the job offer, but had to train a replacement in Copenhagen. Andrea wished him a safe trip. It had been good to see him and spend time with him. The fact that he reminded her of Philip was a comfort to her. He was family and she didn't have much family, at least not males.

When Charles arrived at her house, he wore jeans and a plaid shirt with short sleeves, open at the neck. She'd never seen him dressed like that, and she liked it. He commented on the flowers she and Kristian had planted and asked what kind they were.

"Geraniums and petunias." Andrea pointed them out in case he didn't know the difference.

"It looks terrific. I'd like to have something like that by my patio, but I don't know anything about planting flowers." He was giving her a lead, wasn't he?

"I could help you," she said.

They went to a place where they sold plants, and Andrea told Charles the names of the flowers they saw.

"Are your flowers going to be in a sunny spot or in the shade?" she asked.

"I think it's mostly shade where I want them."

"Then we'll select the impatiens," she said and pointed to them. "They thrive in the shade. As you can see, they come in a variety of colors."

He picked up two flats in assorted colors. They bought planting soil, little spades, and garden gloves. He put everything in the trunk of his car. She was anxious to see where he lived.

"I enjoy being with you, pretty-face," he said, reaching for her hand in the car.

"I enjoy being with you."

He told her he had been to the cemetery on Mother's Day. "

How did your wife die?"

"She had breast cancer."

"Philip had cancer also."

"We've been through some sad times, both of us." Again, he squeezed her hand and she squeezed his. They had so much in common.

He drove up a long driveway. "Here we are," he said. "That's my house." Andrea gasped.

I knew he was well off, but this is a mansion!

"It's a big house," she said. It was an understatement.

"Yes, it's way too big for Todd and me."

"And the lawn…. That's a lot of grass to mow."

"Todd and I take turns. I have a riding mower." Charles drove to the back of the house and unloaded. There was a large patio on the back of the house.

"If I had known about the patio, I would have suggested some potted plants," Andrea said.

"I can get that later. Now, let's plant."

They planted one flat on each side of the steps to the patio.

"This is not enough," Andrea said. "We could have used a dozen flats."

"It will have to do for now," he said. "Let's go in the house. I'm thirsty and you must be too."

They watered the plants and Andrea hosed off her crocs the way she usually did. She put them on the patio and walked into the house barefoot, showing her red toenails. Charles also left his shoes outside the door. Now, she had planted flowers with both Kristian and Charles. It was a husband-and-wife thing to do. She was anxious to see what the mansion looked like on the inside.

"I'll give you a tour of the house," he said. They walked through room after room, Charles in his stocking feet and Andrea barefoot. There were antiques everywhere and a grand piano in the living room. He said he liked the den the best. "I selected the leather furniture for it." Andrea didn't think he cared much for the antique furniture.

They walked by a closed door. "I don't use the master bedroom," he said, pointing to the door. "I sleep upstairs." The next room was the computer room. "Wow, a whole room for computers," Andrea exclaimed.

"Sometimes I need to check up on work on weekends," Charles said, "and Todd uses it for his school work."

Charles cupped her elbow and led her to the large kitchen, where they made iced tea. He put a pitcher and glasses on a tray, "Let's go to the patio and drink it," he said.

"What a beautiful view you have over the valley," Andrea said.

"I like the open spaces."

A car drove up and parked beside the Cadillac. "It's Todd," Charles said. "Now, you'll get to meet him."

The lanky boy dressed in shorts, a T-shirt, and sneakers took two steps at a time up to the patio.

"Howdy!" he said, but when he saw Andrea, he said, "Uh, hello."

"Todd, this is Andrea Holm, the lady I told you about."

"Nice to meet you, ma'am." He bowed his head so his dark brown hair fell down on his forehead. Then he pushed it to the side with one hand and looked at her a second time. His gaze stopped at her red toenails. He resembled his father—the same straight nose, blue eyes, and charming smile.

"We've been planting flowers," Charles said. "Did you see them?"

"Yes, they look nice. Do you have any iced tea for me?"

"Get a glass and help yourself," Charles said.

Todd went to the kitchen and came back with a tumbler. He filled it and sat down with his long. tanned legs stretched out in front of him.

"I hear you're going to Ireland," Andrea said.

"Yes, I've graduated, and I'm looking forward to some free time."

"Ireland should be beautiful in the spring," Andrea said. "I'm sure you'll enjoy it."

"I plan on it. Thanks for the tea. I'm going to use the Internet for awhile, Dad, and check out more sites in Ireland."

"Go ahead, son."

As soon as he had left, Andrea said, "Nice young man."

"Yes, I'll miss him."

"Do you have any Irish relatives?"

"No, but my son-in-law might have relatives over there." He looked at his watch saying, "I'm getting hungry. May I take you out to lunch?"

"I'll accept your offer."

They stood up and brought their glasses to the kitchen. Charles looked into the computer room, saying, "We're going out to eat. Then I'll take Andrea home. You can go to McDonalds if you like."

"Okay, Dad." Todd looked up from his laptop.

"It was nice meeting you, Todd," Andrea said.

Standing up and facing them, he answered, "Yes, ma'am, same here."

Andrea's crocs had dried and she put them on. They admired the flowers they had planted when a big car drove up and a woman stepped out.

"It's my sister-in-law, Susan," Charles said, holding Andrea back with one arm.

"The trouble-maker?"

Charles nodded. He introduced Andrea as his lady friend. That didn't sit well with Susan. She hardly acknowledged Andrea's presence.

"I lost an earring at your party, and I need to find it," Susan said.

"Help yourself. Look around. Todd's inside. We're going out to eat."

"Dressed like that?" Susan looked disapprovingly at them.

"We've been planting flowers," Andrea said as an excuse.

"So I see. Are you a gardener or something?" Andrea gasped at the remark. The woman was vicious.

"That was uncalled for, Susan," Charles said in a sharp tone of voice. "It's not necessary to be a gardener to know how to plant flowers. Not that it's anything wrong with being a gardener." Andrea could tell he was irritated, but so was she.

When they were in the car, Charles told her more about Susan.

"She zeroed in on me right after Elaine had passed away. I was only polite to her. I guess she's lonely, but she's also greedy. Elaine was never like that."

"Susan is right though about one thing," Andrea said, looking down at her old jeans. "I'm not dressed for eating in a restaurant."

"Neither am I. We can go to a casual place, but not as casual as McDonald's, where we might run into Todd and his friends."

Charles seemed anxious to repair the damage Susan had caused. "My other relatives are not at all like her," he said. "You'll like my children and their families. Matt is an attorney and his wife Cindy teaches at the university. They're the parents of the children in the photo in my office."

"Yes, I remember."

"My daughter Linda is an author and she writes novels. You're probably familiar with her books, but I'll let her tell you about the titles."

"I'd like to meet her."

"I'll arrange it. She's married to an Irishman. Well, he was born here to Irish parents. His name is Ed and he owns a real-estate firm. They've two boys. You'll also like my mother. She's a widow and lives in a retirement home in Arlington Heights. She'll like you, I'm sure."

"I'm looking forward to meeting your family. I already like Todd."

"You shouldn't pay attention to Susan. She's only jealous because she doesn't have anyone in her life."

The first thing Andrea did when she came home was to check on her newly planted flowers. She said they looked thirsty.

"Let me do the watering," Charles said. He took the hose and turned it on while she watched. When he was done, she asked if he wanted to come inside. He quickly agreed.

As soon as they were inside the door, he grabbed her and began to caress her. "You look so damn sexy in your jeans," he said. She was surprised.

Is this Mr. Charles Bordeaux, attorney-at-law, behaving like a hormone-crazed boy?

She didn't mind. He pressed her against the wall. They both panted.

"I've been aching for you all day," he said as he rubbed against her.

"Someone might come," Andrea said.

"We can lock the door."

"What about the windows?"

They both jumped when they heard a car in the drive-way.

"It's probably Jessica," Andrea said. She blushed like she had been caught doing something forbidden.

"So much for our romantic moment. Guess we'll have to go outside and look innocent," Charles said in a re-signed voice. They both went outside to greet Jessica.

"Hello, Charles. Sorry, Mom. I didn't know you had company."

"It's alright. We have planted flowers at Charles' place today."

"Your mother is a great gardener," Charles said.

"I know. She's good at a lot of things," Jessica said. "I just wanted to borrow a planter for our balcony."

"There're some in the garage," Andrea said.

Charles' cell phone rang. It was Todd. He needed money to buy something.

"Sorry, Andrea, but Todd needs me, or rather my wallet. I'll call you later."

To Jessica he said, "Good luck with your planter."

When Jessica and Charles had left, Andrea wondered what might have happened if Jessica hadn't come. It would probably happen eventually. She was happy in her knowledge that Charles desired her.

The next morning, Susan called her. How had she gotten hold of her phone number?

"You're probably out after Charles' money," Susan said bluntly.

"I'm not," Andrea said firmly. "I didn't know until yesterday he lived in a mansion. I have to go to work now and I don't have time to talk. Goodbye," she said and hung up. She was upset enough to shake. What a nerve that woman had.

But I can't play into her hands and drop Charles. That's what she wants me to do. I'm not letting her scare me.

Chapter 12

They were sitting on Andrea's patio enjoying the warm summer day when Charles said, "I've something to tell you."

"I've something to tell you, too," Andrea said.

"You go first then."

"Susan called me and said I was after your money."

"I don't put it past her," he said, "but I'm very sorry she bothered you."

"I'm getting a caller ID, and if she calls again, I won't answer."

"Smart girl," Charles said.

"Your turn."

"It's about Susan and her demands. She's hired a lawyer, who stipulates that every piece of furniture, china, crystal, silver, and the antiques that Elaine had inherited from her family should be returned to the family, meaning Susan." Andrea gasped in disbelief.

"But that's not all," Charles added. "She also wants all the presents that Elaine's family gave us. I don't even know what that is."

"It must be upsetting to you. Her demands sound outrageous."

"Elaine wanted everything to go to our children after I'm gone. If it goes to Susan, my children won't get any of it. That's what I'm upset about."

"So you'll challenge her request?"

"Yes, on behalf of my children."

"Why is she doing this?"

"She's afraid I'll remarry." He cocked his head while looking at her. "She's probably deadly afraid I will marry the gardener who was at my house."

Andrea gasped at first, but then she smiled. His statement was both funny and serious. She went along with his teasing.

"A gardener, how awful, an attorney marrying a gardener. It would be unthinkable."

"It depends on the gardener."

In many ways, Andrea thought. She knew one thing with certainty. If she were to marry Charles, she wasn't keen on living with Elaine's family possessions. She'd rather see them divided between Charles' children. Too much money and too many belongings would only cause problems.

"Seriously, did your wife have a last will, Charles?"

"Yes, she did. She gave everything to me. After I'm gone, she stipulated that it should go our children."

"So Susan is challenging Elaine's wishes?"

"Essentially."

"Well, you know about the law, Charles. You'll do what you think is best for your children."

"Do you think it's greedy of me to protect what's mine?"

"Not at all, I have my own house, china, silver, and crystal, and I'd protect what's mine for the sake of my daughter."

"You're so sweet. I hope it works out between us."We are off to a good start."

Except for Susan, Andrea thought.

They decided to forget about Susan and enjoy each other's company. Andrea wondered if Charles was ready for a relationship. He'd probably look at it from a lawyer's point of view.

"This is a hypothetical question, but do you think I should sell my house?" Charles asked.

"It's entirely up to you, of course. I can understand that it feels too big for you, especially with Todd moving out. I would get lost in a house that large." It was a hint that she did not wish to live in his house.

"I know this couple—he was a widower and lived in a big house when he met a divorced lady. She also had a house. Their children were grown. They wished to marry, but couldn't decide in which house to live. Anyway, they sold both of their homes and bought a new one. They thought it was best to start anew."

Was that a hint from Charles?

Charles continued to reminisce. "Elaine never worked outside the home, although I know she contributed as much by taking good care of our home and our children."

Andrea wondered if Charles had something against working wives.

"How do you feel about my working, Charles?"

"It's fine, of course, although I have to admit I'm not fond of you working on weekends, but that's because I can't see you as much as I'd like."

"I don't want to work weekends either. I've never liked it, but it's necessary to have a full-time job in order to get company health insurance."

For a moment, she pictured herself as Charles' wife. She would be on his health insurance and have no financial worries. In reality, she didn't think Charles was ready to get married, and Susan could throw a wedge between them.

"I don't want to cause any problems for you and your family, Charles," she said.

"I know, but with you at my side, I can ride out any problems that come in my way, even Susan."

Andrea moved closer to him, and he reached for her.

"Next weekend, Todd will be in Ireland and we're alone. I'll miss Todd terribly, but I'm glad I have you," Charles said.

"I'm glad to have you." In that moment, Andrea felt more certain about her bond with Charles. He was someone she could share her thoughts with, a man to feel close to and to love. She was ready to let go of her dead husband. He would still be in her heart, but she thought Phil would have approved of Charles. If it worked out between them, she hoped it would not bother Jessica to see her happy with another man. Bob would be jealous, but it couldn't be helped. He deserved a good woman, but that woman was someone else. Kristian had reminded her of Philip, and that's why she had been attracted to him. With Charles, she felt happy.

Charles said he had read the housing ads in the paper. "I'd like to look at some of the homes, just to get a feeling of what's out there."

"Would that be a hypothetical house?"

"We could say that."

"I dreamt last night that we lived in a house with a spare room for Todd," Andrea said. Her face reddened.

"So you had a dream about you and me living together. Were we married?" Charles looked amused.

"I don't think that was part of my dream." Andrea reddened even more and quickly added, "Show me the houses you saw in the paper." He pulled her down on his lap, and they both looked at the ads.

"Here's one in Naperville," Charles said.

"That street has a lot of traffic. A house on a court would be better. Here's one in a good location, but, oh boy, it's so expensive."

"If I sell my place, I'm sure I can afford it."

"It has four bedrooms."

"One could be a den."

"That's true. Do you really think you'll sell your house?"

"Yes, I'm sure of it."

"Let's go and look at it then. I think it's by the golf course."

"You said you play golf."

"I used to."

"We should try it sometime."

Andrea directed Charles to the house. They drove passed it slowly a couple of times. It was on a lovely court with many trees.

"I like it," Charles said. "What about you?"

"It looks good from the outside, but it doesn't matter, because it will be sold quickly."

"There'll be others."

"You said you like open spaces."

"Yes, but a golf course is an open space."

"It's hard to beat the open spaces around your house."

"I know, but I think my house should be occupied by a young family with many children. That reminds me, I have to mow the yard when I get home. It will take me three hours. With Todd gone, I have to mow all that grass by myself unless I hire someone. It will be hard to find someone this time of the year. In the winter, there's the snow. I've contracted a man with a snowplow, but he doesn't always show up before I go to work. There're drawbacks to a big property."

"Next weekend I'm free, and then we can look at more hypothetical houses," Andrea said.

He kissed her tenderly and said, "I'm sorry I have to leave." Andrea was sure he was thinking about continuing where they had left off last time, but he had a lot on his mind, and so did she. Best to clear it all up before they got in any deeper.

As Charles left the living room, he stopped by the piano and played a few bars standing up.

"I know it's out of tune, so you don't have to tell me," Andrea said.

"Nothing that can't be rectified."

So he could play the piano. It was fun to discover new things about Charles.

Would he find a house that he liked? Moving would be a considerable transition for him. Andrea also wondered where that would leave her.

On Sunday morning, Kristian called from Copenhagen while Andrea made coffee.

"It's the first time I get a call from another country," she said. "I know you called Phil sometimes, but .... how's it going for you? When are you coming back?"

"Probably in August?"

"Where would you live?"

"The company will get me a furnished apartment until I can find something more permanent. I'd like to buy a condo. Could you give me an idea of a good area?"

"There're lots of condos here in Naperville, and you'd have the train to downtown. Will you be working downtown?"

"Yes, but I'll be traveling abroad also, and I don't think it's easy to get to O'Hare from Naperville. I might want to live on the north side."

"I'll do some checking for you."

"I'd appreciate it."

Chapter 13

Charles prepared to divide Elaine's heirlooms between his children. Matt and his wife said they would be glad to accept some of the antique furniture. Linda wished to have her mother's jewelry, the antique lamps, the rare books, and some furniture. Charles doubted that Todd would want anything that required extra care while he was at the university, but he would get a piece of antique furniture anyway. It had to be something durable.

Charles had contested Susan's request. As for the good china, crystal, and sterling silver, he stated that those were wedding gifts to both him and Elaine, and that he had added to it. He divided the 24-piece place settings, including the silverware, between his three children. They would get eight place settings each. He would store Todd's for the time being. Having had a piece of each appraised, Charles knew how much they were worth.

Susan would get a painting that he didn't like. She had received as much from her parents as Elaine had, so there was no reason to feeling sorry for her. Susan's request had hastened Charles actions. Whether to sell his house and buy a new one were no longer hypothetical questions. It was what he wanted to do. He went ahead and prepared to sell his home. He bought potted plants and placed them on the patio, as Andrea had suggested.

Then he advertised his home on the Internet as "For Sale by Owner." He knew how much his property was worth because he handled the legal matters of home sales every day.

It didn't take long before he had prospective buyers. He showed the house by appointment only. When he received two bids on the same day, he began to feel uneasy about selling so fast. Although he had talked to Matt and Linda about his plans, he hadn't told Todd that he had the house for sale. He decided to place a call to Todd's cell phone.

When Todd answered, he said, "Hi Todd. It's your dad."

"Is everything all right?"

"Yes, it's fine. How are you and Carl?"

"We're having a great time and go hiking almost every day."

"Good. I just wanted you to know that I'm in the process of selling our home, I didn't want it to be a surprise to you when you come back."

There was a short pause. "Why are you selling it, Dad?"

"Because with you gone, I realize that the house is too big for me alone. I think it should be occupied by a family with children."

"Isn't this a little sudden?"

"I realize it seems like that to you, but I'd rather live in a smaller house. When you come home, you'll be getting ready to leave for the university. The house will still be ours until then. Even if I sell it now, it takes time to close the deal. I can stipulate the date of transfer of the title. You'll have time to select what you want to furnish the apartment."

"That would be great, Dad." Todd paused, and then said, "It will be strange, but where would you live?"

"I'll look for another house, but smaller."

"Well, good luck then."

"Thanks Todd."

Charles looked at the two bids. One was higher. Both prospective buyers had pre-approved financing. He would give the couple with the lowest bid a chance to go higher, and let them think about it until Monday.

Charles and Andrea were on their way to see Linda and Ed.

"I've listed my house and I have prospective buyers already. At the rate this is going, I might be homeless by the end of the summer," Charles said, wiggling his eyebrows.

What does he mean? Andrea felt a little anxious. Charles had a lot happening in his life, and she had to wait and see what the future held for them.

She enjoyed meeting Linda and recognized the titles of the books she had authored. Linda was of average height with dark hair and brown eyes. She looked a little bit French, something she no doubt had inherited from the Bordeaux side of her family. Andrea had met many authors at the bookstore, and she was always curious about how they had become successful.

"What does it take to become a published author?" she asked.

"It requires a lot of work, but I think it's best to start with short stories or articles and see if any publishers are interested. Writing classes can be helpful. I have a degree in Fine Arts, but it's not necessary. I write while the boys are in school. When I have a deadline to meet, I might work 12 hours a day."

"That's a lot," Andrea said.

"Yes, but with no deadlines, I can take a day off which is nice. Ed can do the same. Sometimes he works late and on weekends, and at other times he can take a day off."

Charles told Ed that he was selling his house. "Oh, what prompted this?" Ed asked.

"Todd is moving out, and other things play a role. You know I close sales myself and don't need a realtor."

Andrea saw her chance to ask Ed a question.

"My brother-in-law is looking for a condo on the north side," she said. "Could you recommend an area suitable for a single man who will be working downtown? He wants to be relatively close to O'Hare for his business travels."

"Lincoln Park would probably be the best. It's an older updated neighborhood, where houses are being rebuilt and converted to condos. It's popular among singles and young couples. It's close to downtown and not far from the airport."

"Thanks. I'll tell him."

"I can give you a few examples of what's for sale right now."

"I'd appreciate that." Ed immediately went to his computer and printed out several pages handing them to Andrea.

"You can give him my e-mail address, so he can contact me himself, and I can send him information that way.

Ed had thick brown hair, a square jaw, and a determined look. He gestured a lot when he talked, and pointed in the general direction of Lincoln Park.

Charles looked at Andrea and asked, "Did Kristian decide to move to Chicago?"

"Yes, he's moving as soon as he can get away from his job in Copenhagen."

The house by the golf course had a "Sold" sign outside. Naperville was attractive especially because it had a commuter train to Chicago.

Charles decided to look at new construction in the area. They saw homes at various stages of construction. Most of them had openings where the windows and doors would go, so they could walk in and see the layout. The unfinished homes smelled of plywood.

They looked at a model home that was open for inspection. It had a chandelier high up in the ceiling in the foyer. How would anyone get up there to clean the chandelier and replace the bulbs when they burned out? The layout was open with hardly any doors between the rooms. They went down to the basement that smelled murky.

"It would be better to buy in early spring, Charles said. "We don't know what could happen here when it rains."

"It doesn't smell good," Andrea said. "I don't like the smell."

"Let's go," he said. "I've seen enough houses for today."

In the car, Andrea said, "It would be a lot of work to get a new yard in shape, and it would take years for it to grow. You'd have to plant trees, shrubs, and flowers."

"I don't think I'm up to that."

They stood outside Andrea's house.

"Your house is the right size. Your yard is beautiful. Not that much grass to mow. It's the best one I've seen all day," Charles said with a grin.

What was he thinking?

"I like it," she said.

She kicked off her shoes in the hallway. Later, she rested her legs on an ottoman in the living room. Charles brought her a drink. It was perfect.

We could live separately and be happy.

On Monday, Charles had higher bids from both prospective buyers. On Wednesday, he accepted the bid from the couple with the most children. He was satisfied and celebrated by taking Andrea out to dinner on Wednesday night.

"Doesn't it feel strange to sell your home?" she asked.

"Once I've come to the decision, it's almost a relief. It belongs to my former life. Many memories are connected with that house, but I'll always have the memories. No one can take those away from me. All three children grew up there. The problem is that Elaine and I collected too many material things. It will be hard to divide them fairly. Then I'll have to decide what to do with the rest."

Andrea's mind worked in two directions, the theoretical and the practical. Was Charles planning his future with her or not? She could only talk about the practical aspect of what he was doing.

"You could have an estate sale and sell what your children don't want, except for what you plan to keep, of course."

"I suppose so. Half of the proceeds of everything I sell, including the house, will go into a trust fund for my kids as their mother's inheritance."

"Downsizing can be difficult," she said.

"But it can also be a good idea. At the end of our lives, we can't take anything with us."

"That's so true."

Andrea could still not be certain about Charles' intentions. He had dropped hints, but that's all.

Kristian called and began by saying, "How's my favorite sister-in-law?"

"I don't think you have more than one sister-in-law," she said.

"Not yet, but I might have later. I've got big news for you. My fiancée and I are together again. In order for her to get a visa to the U.S., we need to marry here in Denmark."

"Congratulations, Kristian. That's good news." Andrea was surprised but also relieved.

"Would you be interested in coming to my wedding?"

"I'd love to, but I can't get time off from work," Andrea said. "Jessica should be able to get away. When is it?"

"In July, I'll call her and ask her myself."

"By the way, I found out that Lincoln Park would be a good area for you to buy a condo. Charles' son-in-law is in real estate, and he recommended it for singles and young couples. Evidently, it's a rejuvenated community with lots of restaurants."

"I know it's close to downtown and to the lake," Kristian said. "It sounds good to me."

"I can give you the contact information to Ed's firm. Then you can take it from there. Jessica has e-mail."

"Great. I'll call Jessica and invite her to my wedding, and I can get her e-mail address at the same time. She said she'd like to visit Denmark."

Andrea sat down and waited for Jessica to call her. If Kristian had reached her on the phone, it won't take long. Jessica would be happy to attend Kristian's wedding.

Andrea was right. It didn't take long for Jessica to call.

"Mom, I'm so excited I can hardly breathe. I'm so sorry you can't come with me to Copenhagen. Jason can't either, but I can go alone."

"I'm so happy for you. I've always wanted to see Denmark, but I can't go. Your dad said he would take me to both Denmark and Sweden when he retired, but, well, you know what happened."

"I'll get online and check the airline prices in July. It will be the high season for Europe and the most expensive."

"I'd be glad to pay for your ticket." Andrea knew that teachers didn't make much money.

"Well, perhaps half, I'll get back to you, Mom."

Andrea could put her temporary infatuation with Kristian to rest. There would be no problems in the future. He would have a wife.

And hopefully, I'll have a husband. I can stop chasing Philip's ghost. Jessica is a descendant of the Holm family. She should go to Copenhagen.

It was Sunday morning and Andrea was frying bacon and scrambling eggs. The fan hummed. She didn't hear Charles walking into her kitchen, but felt his presence before he kissed her on her neck and put his arms around her.

"It smells good in here," he said. Last night was wonderful. Now, I'm hungry."

She could smell her mouthwash on his breath. He had not planned to spend the night, so he hadn't brought anything of his own. White stubble covered his chin. He still looked great and masculine.

"Now, we're a couple," she said as she turned around to kiss him.

"Yes, now we're a couple."

Andrea had no regrets. She was sure of her love for him. They had professed their love for each other. What could be better than waking up in Charles' arms? She was only sorry she had to be at work at 1:00 o'clock.

Andrea thought that Charles looked thoughtful at the breakfast table. "A penny for your thought, honey," she said.

"I still know so little about you," he said. "When is your birthday?"

"It's in two weeks, June 25. I don't have to work that weekend," she hinted.

"That's good. I'm free, too. Next weekend is Father's Day, and the children will be coming, all except Todd."

He picked up a piece of bacon and chewed on it.

"I understand."

"I'll make it up to you. Do you want to go away for your birthday? We could fly to New York."

Now, that was a surprise move by Charles. Andrea almost choked on her coffee.

"Are you alright?" he asked.

"Yes, that would be wonderful." She felt like jumping with joy.

"I'll get the tickets then. New York will be a special place for your birthday."

"Very special. When is your birthday, Charles?"

"February 14, Valentines' Day."

"That's easy to remember."

Little by little, they were finding out more about each other.

Chapter 14

Andrea was ready with her overnight bag when Charles drove up her driveway at six o'clock in the morning.

"Happy birthday, darling! Here's your first birthday kiss."

Andrea enjoyed the early morning kiss and a whiff of his aftershave before they sat down in the car heading for O'Hare Airport. Charles described the security at the airport, explaining that they would have to take their shoes off before going through screening. Andrea had not flown since it became mandatory.

She told Charles about Kristian's upcoming marriage in Copenhagen and that Jessica would attend.

"I didn't know Kristian had a girlfriend, but I shouldn't be surprised. Jessica will love going to Copenhagen, I'm sure."

"For some reason Kristian and Marie broke off their first engagement, but I'm glad they're together again. After their marriage, Marie will get her visa and they'll move to Chicago. I just found out." Andrea thought that everything had worked out for the best.

As they approached the airport, she observed the planes coming in for landing and departures. Charles drove to the long-term parking lot and parked the car, and from there they took the airport train to the terminal. He knew what to do, and Andrea just followed him. How fortunate she was to have found a man who was not only wonderful, but also well off economically. She loved his generous birthday gift. It was her lucky day.

Andrea looked down at New York City from the air and the outline of Manhattan before the big jet began its abrupt descent to La Guardia Airport in Queens. Her ears hurt, and she braced herself for the landing. She clutched Charles' hand. The wheels touched the ground fast and hard. Will the plane stop in time? Charles turned to look at her. Seeing her scared face, he put one arm around her. She drew a long breath when the plane slowed. "I'm glad to be on the ground," she said. She shook her head until her ears popped.

"The descent here is always steep," Charles said. "It's a small airfield with lots of buildings and water nearby."

"It was scary. The pilots have to be very skillful."

They rolled their carry-on luggage with them as they exited the airport. Charles guided Andrea to the van that would take them to their hotel. He said they would be close to Times Square, Broadway, and Central Park. Andrea had already decided what she wanted to see: Empire State Building, the site of the World Trade Center, where the two towers had stood before they were destroyed on 9/11, and the Broadway musical, *Mamma Mia*. If time allowed, she wanted to go to the United Nations and the Rockefeller Center.

On their way to the city, Andrea looked around, but saw only cars and the closest buildings. She had never been to New York City before and was very excited. Best of all, she was there with Charles.

From their hotel room, she looked down on the traffic on Fifth Avenue far below their window. Charles came up behind her and drew her close. She turned and accepted his welcome-to-New York kiss.

He suggested that they go to Empire State Building while the weather was clear and sunny. They rode the elevator to the top and enjoyed a fantastic view of the city. They looked at the sprawling boroughs in all directions surrounded by water. "It's breathtaking," Andrea said.

"I think you're taking my breath away, pretty-face," Charles said. What he did next astonished Andrea. He took out a small, black box from his inside pocket, looked into her eyes and asked, "Will you marry me, Andrea?"

Andrea's mouth fell and her eyes opened wide. Her body tingled all the way to her tippy toes. Her knees threatened to buckle under her.

"Yes, yes, I'll be glad to marry you." She leaned into him for support and he lifted her off the floor.

"Thank you, darling. I'm sorry I couldn't go down on one knee on this dirty floor, but I love you so much and I want you to be my wife." Slowly he put her down to put the ring on her finger. "Hope that this will fit you, my darling," he said.

Andrea admired the ring and looked up at him with shining eyes. "I love you and I'll be honored to be your wife." Tears came to her eyes as she stretched out her manicured hand, moved her sapphire ring to the other hand, and let Charles slide his ring in its place.

"It's beautiful, Charles. Thank you for the ring, and again thank you for crashing into my car, so we could meet. I couldn't be happier."

"It was meant to be." Charles said, once again lifting her from the floor. They kissed and held each other tightly.

"We'll always remember this place and this moment," Andrea said. Her voice choked with emotions. He had planned this as a surprise and she had been oblivious.

"How far back did you plan this, Charles?" Her voice rose in anticipation of his answer.

Charles became serious. "I've known for some time that I wanted to marry you, and when you mentioned your birthday, I decided it would be a good time to propose," he said.

"And all the while, you let me think you were buying a house for yourself."

"The truth is that all along I pictured you in the homes we saw, and none of them was good enough for you."

"I've pictured you in my house as my husband."

"I appreciate that, darling. It might be the best solution."

"I think so, too."

"May I take a snapshot of my fiancée? I have my digital camera with me. Look happy," he said as he pointed the camera at her.

"The problem is that I'm so happy I want to cry. I want you to be with me in the picture."

"Alright, we'll do it like this." He hugged her from the side with one arm and held the camera with his free hand, snapping close-up pictures of them.

"Let me see, please," she said. Charles showed her and commented, "It worked. We look very happy."

"Yes, we do, and we are."

"Do you want to go to our room and rest for awhile before we take in *Mamma Mia* tonight?"

"Yes." She still couldn't believe she was engaged for the second time in her life.

Back at their hotel, they stripped off their traveling clothes and met in the king-sized bed. Andrea wore her ring and nothing else. None of the relatives or family members mattered anymore. It was only the two of them, away from home, away from the attorney's office and the bookstore, away from Susan and any looming troubles. They were in New York City, where their love had no bounds. They would marry and live their own lives, their own way, together, wherever, but forever.

"You're the fulfillment of my life, darling," Charles said.

"I feel the same way," Andrea whispered.

All her anxieties were gone, and she was completely relaxed.

Dressing in evening clothes, they went to see the *Mamma Mia* musical on Broadway. Enjoying the show, they sang along with the catchy tunes, *Money, Money, Money*, and *Thanks for the Music.*

The yellow cabs came in a steady stream to pick up people who had been to the shows, but Charles and Andrea walked as they made their way to a restaurant for a combined birthday and engagement dinner. Charles had made the reservation in advance.

Seated by the table, with the waiter pouring the champagne, Andrea said, "You've thought of everything, Charles."

"To your birthday, darling."

"To our engagement," she answered.

"May it not last too long?" Charles said with a big grin on his face.

"What do you mean?"

"I don't believe in long engagements, darling. I want to marry you as soon as possible."

"I feel like the luckiest woman in the world."

"You've made me a very happy man."

"It's a very happy birthday for me, the best one in years."

They dined on lobster tail, Andrea's favorite, but a rare luxury. As they walked back to the hotel, she thought about her first engagement. Philip had been young and poor. He didn't even own a car, but rode a motorcycle. She smiled at the comparison. It was definitely more comfortable the second time around.

Resting in Charles' arms, Andrea asked. "Do I please you the way I should?"

"You do. I've heard that women over fifty are fantastic lovers, and that is certainly true of you."

"I'm glad. Thank you for not saying 'older women.' I enjoy intimacy more than I ever did. I never thought I'd be falling in love after 50."

Charles leaned on one elbow and said, "50 is only a number. It's how you feel that matters. What kind of wedding do you want, darling?"

"A simple one, we could get be married by a judge with only family present, and no Susan, please."

"She won't be invited," Charles said. "As for the ceremony, I know a good judge. Do you want to set a date?"

"Let's wait until Todd has settled down at college. You don't want to upset his life too much. Everything has happened so fast," Andrea said.

"I agree. Where should we go on our honeymoon?"

"I feel like this is our honeymoon."

"I do, too, but I think we should go out of the country for our real honeymoon. What about a Greek Island like the one in the musical?"

"It would be nice, but I've always wanted to see Paris."

"Then we'll go to Paris. We can go to a Greek island in the winter when it's cold here. My ancestors came from France."

"And that's why your name is Bordeaux?"

"Yes, and it will be your name, unless you want to keep your present one."

Do I want to change my name? I've always liked my short surname.

"Hmm. Isn't Bordeaux a city in France?" she asked.

"Yes, it's a port city in the southwestern part."

"Can we go there?" Andrea realized she sounded like a kid asking for more candy.

"I can't see why not, but I want to show you Paris first. It's fantastic."

"I'm sure it is. You're so good to me."

Despite the traffic and noise of the city, they slept well in each other's arms.

"Good morning, beautiful." Charles tickled Andrea under her chin.

"Good morning. What happened to pretty-face?"

"She's still there, but I have more names for you now. One of them is fiancée."

"And then I'll be your wife."

"I can't wait to have you as my wife."

"And you'll be my husband."

"Yes, I like that, too. It's good that I didn't have to wait for all the benefits though."

"At our age, we shouldn't have to."

"Now, I want another taste of our old-age benefit."

"Charles, your jokes are terrible, but I love you."

They had breakfast in the hotel restaurant when Charles suggested they take one of the sightseeing tours the hotel recommended. A bus would pick them up outside the hotel, and they would get to see more sights than they could on their own. Andrea agreed.

The group stood at the site of the World Trade Center. It was free of debris, but the building of the new tower had not started.

"I knew a man who was killed here when the towers collapsed," Charles said.

"I'm sorry. The whole thing was so awful. Those killed were in their best years. They were educated, successful contributors to society, and they had families, who depended on their support. What a tragedy."

The tour leader suggested a minute of silence, and everyone in the group bowed their heads while the city was far from quiet.

When they passed the Empire State Building, Charles and Andrea looked at each other. "We know about that one, don't we darling?" Charles said. Andrea nodded while looking at her ring that sparkled in the sunlight from the bus window. The ring had a large square diamond in the center and smaller ones along the sides. Charles had made a good selection.

It must have cost a lot. The ring that Philip gave me had only a small diamond but it was still dear to me.

She felt guilty for having made the comparison. It was not fair. Times had changed, and Charles could afford a more expensive ring.

Forgive me Phil for starting a new life.

The bus stopped at the Rockefeller Center and the United Nations so they could disembark and take pictures. Charles brought out his digital camera and snapped a few pictures with Andrea in the foreground with the flags of many nations in the background.

Once they were back at the hotel again, they had time for lunch and a short stroll in Central Park before they boarded a van headed for La Guardia and their flight back to Chicago. Andrea couldn't have been happier about her weekend and the surprise engagement.

Chapter 15

Andrea could hardly wait to call Nana and Jessica to tell them the big news. Of course, she had to call her sisters too. They were all surprised and amazed. When they heard that it happened in New York, they were even more amazed.

"How could you keep this from us?" they asked. Her sisters wanted to know when they could meet the wondrous man. "When is the wedding? Where will you live?" The questions kept coming. Nancy, who was divorced, said she would like to meet someone like Charles. Kathy had made a good first match, but her husband had been married before. Kathy always said she was the wicked stepmother.

Andrea explained that Charles had surprised her with the proposal.

"That's so awesome. I'd like to throw an engagement party for you," Kathy said.

"It's not necessary."

"I know, but I'll talk to Roger and Nancy about it, and call you back. Again, congrats, sis!"

The next morning, Andrea faced Bob and Trudy at the store. Trudy saw the sparkling diamond ring right away.

"Congratulations!" she said as she admired Andrea's ring. "Have you set a date?"

"Not exactly."

"I know someone who would love to have your job. Surely you'll not work after you marry an attorney?"

"I don't know yet what I'm going to do. Perhaps I'll work part time."

When Bob approached them, Trudy said, "Look, Andrea is engaged to Charles."

Bob looked sideways at her and said, "I'm happy for you, Andrea. I don't know Charles, but he is a lucky man."

"Thank you, Bob. I'll let you know what I decide about my job." She still floated on air.

In the evening, Andrea had several recordings on her answering machine. Kathy asked if the evening before Fourth of July would be good for the party at her place. They would shoot off some fireworks. Nancy had called and said she would help Kathy with the party.

As soon as she had listened to her sisters' messages, the phone rang. It was Charles.

"How's is my darling fiancée today?"

"It seems our engagement has created quite a stir in my family, Charles."

"How so?"

"My sisters want to throw an engagement party for us on the evening before Fourth of July. Kathy and Roger live in Evanston on the lake, and Nancy lives in Wilmette. The party will be at Kathy's. We can be outside on their patio if the weather allows."

"Will I be invited?"

"Of course you're invited!"

"No gifts, I hope."

"I'll make that clear."

"Well then, I'd be glad to accompany you."

"It will be an informal cookout party. Everyone will wear shorts."

"So they live on the lake. What's Kathy's husband doing?"

"He's an investment broker. Kathy volunteers in the community and at Northwestern University—with exchange students, and such, and the Hospital Auxiliary. She also plays a lot of golf. Roger is a fan of the Northwestern football team, so they go to all the games."

"Then they don't have many winning games to celebrate."

"I know, but they go anyway."

"I'd like to meet your relatives."

"That's the purpose of the party."

"Alright then, darling. Now, I have something to ask of you."

"And what's that?"

"I'm invited to a cocktail party on July 9th, and I hate to go alone to those things. Would you accompany me, please?"

"Of course, I will, honey."

"I'd be proud to introduce you to my colleagues as my fiancée."

I should have bought that cocktail dress when I had the chance. Hope it's still there.

"It will be a dress-up affair, I suppose?"

"Yes, but not overly so, I'll be wearing a dark suit."

On her next day off from work, Andrea drove to the boutique where she had seen the black cocktail dress. The salesclerk remembered her and said, "I'm sorry, but I no longer have that dress, but I have a red one."

"Uh, a red one?"

"It would be a better color on you, especially in the summer. I'll bring it so that you can try it on."

The sleeveless dress was cut very low in the front.

"I don't know if I can wear this," Andrea said.

"Try it on and we'll see."

In the fitting room, Andrea pulled down the long zipper of the red dress and stepped into it. She could barely pull the zipper all the way up. The skirt was shorter than she normally wore and her bra was showing.

"How does it fit?" the salesclerk asked through the closed door.

"I don't have the right bra for it," Andrea said as she opened the door.

"We can fix that. We carry bras. I'll bring you one."

While Andrea waited for another bra, she looked at the price tag. The original price was high, but it had been marked down.

"Do you think this dress would be alright for a cocktail party?" she asked the clerk when she returned. "I thought cocktail dresses were black."

"They come in all colors. Here, try on this bra. I think it will fit you and the dress."

The bra was red. She had never owned a red bra. She put it on and saw that it fit nicely underneath the dress.

"I don't know if I'll feel comfortable showing so much cleavage," she said as she opened the door.

"Are you going with someone to the party?"

"My fiancé." It was still new to her to say the word, but she liked it.

"He'll love it."

"I want to make a good impression on his colleagues as well."

"You will. I sell many dresses that have more cleavage. It's the latest style. I have red panties to go with the red bra, and I could give you a good deal if you buy all three."

The lingerie costs almost as much as the dress, but Charles is worth the spending spree. Andrea charged it.

With the dress bag and a small bag for the lingerie, she headed to Jessica's apartment. She was anxious to hear what her daughter would say about the dress. School was out for the summer and Jessica did computer work at home for Jason.

"I see you've been shopping," Jessica said. "But first I want to see your engagement ring." Andrea stretched out her left hand while holding the bags in her right.

"Oh, Mom, it's beautiful. Only older men can afford a ring like that. When is the wedding?"

"We haven't set a date yet, but when we do, do you think you could be one of our witnesses?"

"I never thought I would be a witness at your wedding, Mom, but of course, I'd be glad to. What kind of dress did you buy this time?"

"I'm going to a cocktail party with Charles, so I went back to the boutique to take another look at the black dress we saw last time. But it was gone, and this is what I bought instead." She pulled off the bag, and Jessica ogled the dress.

"Wow, Mom, this is really something. Put it on so I can see how it looks on you."

"I can take it back if you think it's too much for me."

Andrea put on her new red bra before she modeled the dress for her daughter.

"Well, you look like a completely different woman, Mom."

"I need to look good when I meet Charles' executive friends."

"I think they'll say you're hot, Mom."

"So you think it's too much?"

"No, I don't. At least your back is covered. You want to look chic for a party like that. I'd say, keep it."

"Thank you, Jessica."

"I'll put the teakettle on and then you can tell me about New York."

Andrea felt good about the dress. She was happy and she couldn't hide it from Jessica or anyone else. She told her daughter about the proposal at the Empire State Building.

"That's so romantic," Jessica said. They chatted happily while they drank the tea. Jessica wanted to know what kind of marriage ceremony they would have.

"I haven't thought about that yet. A judge will marry us, so I suppose I should wear a light suit."

"It would be perfect."

"And then we're going to Paris on our honeymoon."

"Paris! You're so lucky, Mom. Did you get your passport?"

"Not yet, but I have applied for one. Do you have one for your trip to Denmark?"

"I have a valid passport." Jessica looked at her mother's hair and said, "You should let it grow longer for your wedding."

"That's what I'm planning. By the way, there will be an engagement party at Kathy's the day before the Fourth of July. Can you and Jason come?"

"Sorry, but I'm going to Kristian's wedding in Copenhagen."

"In my excitement I forgot about that. Should I send a wedding present with you, or should I wait until they come here?"

"I think we should wait until they come here. Then they won't have to move the gifts."

"Good idea. I'm looking forward to hearing all about it."

I'm glad that Jessica has a trip to plan. It will take her mind off my wedding that must have been a surprise to her.

131

Chapter 16

Andrea stood in the shower and let her hands run over her breasts. She stopped. What was that? She felt a pea-sized lump. It hadn't been there before. Terrified, she grabbed a towel and dried herself. She looked at her breasts in the mirror. There was no outward change, but the lump was still there. She had to call her doctor right away. Breast cancer would ruin everything. Would Charles stay with her? He had lost his first wife to breast cancer.

Her hands shook as she dialed the number to her doctor and asked to talk to the nurse. When the nurse heard about the lump, she said that Andrea could come at any time the same day.

"I'll come right away," she said.

As she drove to the doctors office horrible thoughts crossed her mind—breast removal, chemo, losing her hair, vomiting.

I can't wear my red dress. I can't marry. I'd have to set Charles free. I might die. I might die before my mother.

The doctor examined her and ordered a mammogram for the next day. She said that a lump didn't have to mean cancer.

"You don't have any breast cancer in your family, do you?"

"Not that I know."

"You might not need a biopsy. Try to calm down."

Andrea was in a daze when she drove up her driveway. She couldn't tell Charles. Why scare him if it was nothing.

The only person I can tell is Nana. Bless her. She's home most of the time and easy to reach on he phone.

Nana said the same as the doctor. "No need to worry at this point. It's probably nothing. Many women have nodules in their breasts."

"But Kathy and Roger are throwing an engagement party for us on July 3rd. Then on July 9th, I'm going with Charles to a cocktail party. I've already bought a dress."

"I'm sure you can attend those events. Even if your doctor recommends a biopsy, the procedure is done with local anesthesia, and you should be home in an hour or so. I have friends who have had it done. If I were you, I wouldn't tell anybody else about it until you know what you're dealing with."

"Thanks, Nana. I'm going to work now. It will give me something else to think about. Could you come on Wednesday, so I'll have a legit reason for not seeing Charles?"

"Of course, honey. I'll be there."

Thank God for mothers. Charles would have known that something was wrong. Nana would calm her down.

Andrea couldn't sleep. Her mammogram was in the morning. How soon would they know the results? When Charles called in the evening, he told her he'd be in court on Wednesday and apologized for not having time to see her.

"It's all right, Charles. My mother is coming, and she will stay over like she usually does."

"Then I won't feel so bad. I need to prepare for the court case. You take care of yourself, darling. We'll talk on Thursday and make plans for Saturday."

Andrea had trouble holding back her tears. "I love you," she said.

"And I love you."

Will he love me if I lose a breast and have to take chemo and radiation? I could lose my hair and eyebrows and look awful? No, I can't put him through that. He has already gone through all that with his first wife. I'd have to break up with him, but how can I do that when I love him so much?

Dear God, let it not be cancer. Why is it that people turn to God when things get a little rough? Why would God listen to me now? I prayed when Philip was sick, and he still died.

Andrea was exhausted. Her mother would come in the morning. With that thought, she finally went to sleep.

They waited for the results of the mammogram at home. Her mother was with her. Waiting alone would have been difficult.

"Let's do something so time will go faster," Nana said. "How about baking cookies? It's good for the soul."

"All right, what kind of cookies? I don't know if I have the ingredients we need."

Andrea thought about all the Swedish cookie recipes she'd gotten from Nana, and now when Nana wanted to bake, there wasn't enough butter in the refrigerator.

Nana checked the cupboards. "Well, you have brownie mix. It would be easy."

"So we'll have brownies for comfort if the news is bad."

"And when the news is good, we can celebrate with brownies."

Andrea took out a mixing bowl and the brownie pan. She turned the oven on. Mother was right as always. It was good to have something to do.

When the brownies were in the oven and Nana washed the mixing bowl, the phone rang. Andrea hurried to answer. It was her doctor.

"Andrea, the nodule looks like it's benign. We could do another mammogram in six months and see if it has changed, or we could do a biopsy right away. Which would you prefer?"

"I want to have the biopsy done right away. I'm supposed to get married in a few weeks. If it's malignant, I'll postpone the wedding." She looked at Nana as she said it. "How soon can I have the biopsy?"

The doctor didn't know. She said that many doctors went on vacation around the Fourth of July, but she would call as soon as she knew the date.

"So the waiting isn't over," Andrea said.

"I didn't think so, but the brownies are done, and I'm sure they will taste good with coffee."

"I'm glad you're here with me, Nana. It would be hard to do all this waiting by myself."

"That's what mothers are for."

Daughters should be equally devoted, Andrea thought. She'd remember that in the future.

"The brownies are good, but how many calories are there in one brownie? Probably about three hundred," Andrea said as she bit into one.

"You're burning calories just by worrying, honey."

"I should go out and mow the lawn. Would you watch the phone for me, Nana?"

"Of course, honey."

Andrea watered the flowers when Nana came outside carrying the phone. "It's your doctor," she said.

Andrea listened intently to the doctor, who said she couldn't get an appointment for the biopsy until July 12th and added, "I don't think you've anything to worry about. The nodule might just be the result of your accident when your breasts were compressed. Go ahead and enjoy the Fourth of July."

Andrea turned to Nana and told her what the doctor had said.

"It makes sense. So will you relax now?"

"Yes, I'll try."

"I'll come back on July 12th. You'll need someone to drive you."

"Thanks, Nana. I can always depend on you. I don't want you to tell Nancy and Kathy. They might spill it at the party. Don't tell Jessica or anyone else either."

"I won't say a peep."

Andrea continued to sprinkle water on her new plants.

"Your flowers are pretty," Nana said.

"They're coming along. I hope Charles is watering his. I helped him plant them."

"And he's going to sell his house, you said?"

"That's what he says. Nana, just think! What if Charles sells his house and it turns out I have cancer? I can't stop him now, and if he sells it, he won't have a place to live if we don't get married."

"Was he going to live with you? Is that what you have planned?"

"Yes, that's what we decided, but if I have cancer, I'll cancel the wedding. I don't want Charles to have another wife with cancer."

"It should be up to him to decide, but I don't think you have cancer. Call it a mother's intuition."

"Hope you're right."

"Perhaps we could take home a movie and watch tonight," Nana suggested. "But first, let's sit down here on the patio and talk," she said. "I want to suggest I give a dinner at a restaurant for our closest relatives after your wedding ceremony."

"If we are wed, that is. I will not set a date yet."

"I understand, honey."

"Please don't send out any invitations."

"As you wish, Andrea, it will be only family. We don't need any written invitations."

Andrea was afraid that her marriage would cost Nana money that she might need for a nursing home later on. Perhaps she could make it up to her if she was married to Charles.

The movie, *Titanic*, that Andrea rented put her problems in perspective. Her situation seemed trivial in comparison with all the loss of life from the tragic sinking.

Chapter 17

Andrea took one day at the time and tried not to worry about her upcoming procedure. She checked her breast every day and thought that the lump was getting smaller. Perhaps it was going away. If the lump was caused by the accident, it might. It was wishful thinking but better than the alternative. She didn't say anything to Charles about it, because she was determined to treasure every minute they had together.

On Saturday, he came dressed in shorts, carrying an overnight bag, and she welcomed him with a warm kiss. He reached into his bag and took out an envelope. "I had some prints made for you," he said.

"Are they from New York?" Andrea's voice rose in anticipation.

"Yes, darling, they're from New York."

She opened the envelope and exclaimed, "Oh, here we're at the Empire State Building! I look so small beside you."

"You look happy, and so do I."

"I think this one is the best," she said. Both of them were looking down on the ring on Andrea's hand.

"So that will be our official engagement picture then."

"I'll frame it." Andrea looked at the rest of the pictures from the United Nations with all nations' flags in the background and outside the Rockefeller Center.

"I see the Swedish flag at the U.N.," Andrea said, "and the Danish, too."

"I tried to get them in the background, and I guess I was successful."

"We had a wonderful time," she said. Charles agreed wholeheartedly.

Andrea wanted to make the most of all their weekends. More than once, she took the initiative to their intimate moments, and Charles loved it. They both loved it, but they also talked and shared their thoughts, everything except Andrea's fear of cancer.

"What did you do last Wednesday when I was in court?" he asked.

"Nana and I saw the movie *Titanic.*"

"Did you like it?"

"It was scary, but I liked it."

"It's a love story with a sad ending."

"Yes, but not only because the hero dies in the movie. In reality, more than 1,500 people lost their lives. Nana said that the Lord's Prayer was recited in Swedish in the movie, so there must have been many Swedes on board."

"There were people of many different nationalities. I saw the Titanic exhibit when it was at the Museum of Science and Industry. I think it was in 2000," Charles said.

"I'm sorry I missed it."

"I believe the exhibit is in Denver now, and that's where my brother lives. We could go there and see it."

"I'd love to."

If I don't have cancer, that is.

On Sunday afternoon, they drove to Evanston for the party at Kathy and Roger's place on the lake.

"Do I need to activate the GPS?" Charles asked.

"No, I know the way. We can take the Interstate north or we can go to Lake Shore Drive.

"Let's go along Lake Michigan."

Andrea put her hand on his bare thigh, and at once, he reached toward her legs that were also bare.

"We can't get too excited in the car," she said.

"I know, but it feels good to touch."

Andrea told him about her mother's wish to give a small dinner after their wedding ceremony.

"It's nice of her to offer."

"But I told her I don't want any invitations sent out. It's for family only."

"It's your choice to make, but we need to decide who our witnesses should be."

"Jessica has already agreed, and perhaps your eldest son, Matt?"

"I'll ask Matt then. He seems to be okay with my marrying again."

As they drove north on Lake Shore Drive they saw many sailboats on the lake. "Chicago has a beautiful lake shore," Charles said. "I know people who own sailboats, and perhaps we could go out with them sometimes."

"Roger and Kathy have a speedboat, but I've never been on a sailboat," Andrea said.

Arriving at the party, they were greeted by applause.

"Welcome, you're the honored guests," Kathy said. She and Nancy hugged Andrea, and Charles pressed their hands as they congratulated him on the engagement. Andrea could tell that her sisters approved of her choice of a future husband.

"I can see the resemblance between you sisters," Charles said. "The corners of their mouths turn up the same as yours," he whispered to Andrea.

Roger wore a ball cap to protect his bald head from the sun. He kissed Andrea, congratulated them both, and shook Charles' hand. He was the same height as Charles but much thinner.

"You've a nice place here," Charles said.

"We love it, especially in the summer. The sand dunes are right below. Come and meet our other guests."

Charles was good at engaging people in conversations. He repeated their names and observed their looks. Then he asked questions to show he was interested in them. Andrea helped him out by telling him more. Some of the guests were neighbors. One neighbor acted as bartender and another helped with the grilling. Roger offered a toast to the newly engaged couple.

Andrea asked Kathy if she needed help with anything.

"No, you're a guest, but I'd like to talk with you in the kitchen." Charles was busy talking with Roger, so she went with Kathy.

"He's gorgeous," Kathy whispered. Nancy was in the kitchen putting a salad together. She was the shortest of the sisters and Kathy the tallest. Kathy had a deep suntan from many days at the golf course. Her hair was rather long and sun-bleached.

"You're so lucky, sis," Nancy said. "Now, tell us about your engagement and upcoming wedding."

"We can't be away from the other guests that long," Andrea said, smiling broadly.

"Alright, let's go out there and talk at one of the tables," Nancy said. "I'll put the salad in the fridge."

"If you can't tell us the date, at least you can tell us if you'll have a reception after the ceremony."

"It's going to be a dinner," Andrea said. "Nana has offered to arrange it. You didn't forget to invite her to come here today, did you?"

"No, I invited her, but as usual she didn't want to drive that far," Kathy said. "And Jessica was going to Copenhagen, so she couldn't take her." Andrea felt guilty about not having offered Nana a ride.

"Are you going to move into Charles' house after you two are married?" Nancy asked.

"No, he's selling his house. We don't need a big home," Andrea said.

Charles approached. "What are you ladies talking about?" he asked.

"Your wedding," Kathy said. "What else?"

Charles tucked his arm under Andrea's.

"It will be very simple," he said. "Then we'll go to Paris on our honeymoon."

"P a r i s!" Kathy and Nancy said in unison.

They were interrupted by Roger's announcement that the food was ready. "Did you hear that, Roger? They're going to Paris on their honeymoon." Kathy said.

"I heard."

While they ate, Charles talked with Nancy and found out what her interests were. She was a schoolteacher, and talked and acted like one. Her favorite hobby was reading. Her dark, short hair reminded Charles of when Andrea had cut her hair short.

"I see there are teenagers here. Are any of them yours?"

"Well, the two girls are mine, and the two boys are Kathy's. Kathy also has three grown stepdaughters, but they're married and living elsewhere."

After they had eaten and the sun began to set, they walked down to the beach to watch the fireworks. The teenagers led the way, carrying fireworks of their own. They ran across the dunes with ease, while the adults stumbled and sank down in the sand. Andrea held on to Charles' arm. Roger announced that the first rocket was for the newly engaged couple.

"Hope it isn't a dud," Charles said. But it wasn't, it was beautiful and colorful. Everyone applauded as it burst open high above.

"It's a good omen," Andrea said, and shrugged off the thought of cancer.

When they had set off all their own fireworks, they watched the neighbors' displays. The Chicago fireworks would go on the next day on Independence Day. They lumbered up to the house and emptied their shoes of sand.

As Charles and Andrea drove home, they saw fireworks lighting up the sky in the neighborhoods that they passed. Back home in Naperville, they heard the crackling noise of celebration until long after midnight.

Andrea enjoyed her weekend with Charles until he said he had to go home and mow the lawn. Standing in her driveway, Andrea waved to him as he left. It was getting harder and harder to part. How in the world would she be able to say a final goodbye to him if it turned out that she had cancer?

Chapter 18

The next time Andrea worked at the store she asked Trudy if she could fill in for her for a couple of hours on Saturday afternoon so she could get ready for the cocktail party.

"I can do that, and if you need more time off before your wedding, I'll take those hours also."

"I appreciate that very much. I need a day off on Monday, July 12. Could you work my hours then?"

"I could do a full day."

"Terrific." With very few customers, they had time to talk. The weather was nice, and people wanted to be outside. Since Bob wasn't in the store, they didn't have to move books or work on displays. Andrea picked up a magazine and read about weddings. They were the kind with young brides, size zero.

Why didn't the magazines feature anything for mature brides?

Andrea mentioned it to Trudy, and she thought it was because it wouldn't sell enough magazines.

"You're probably right." Trudy was a full-bodied woman. "I'm glad I'm already married," she said, "but I saw an article about a celebrity woman who had married in her fifties. Let's see if I can find it." Trudy went through the display, and found it. "Here it is," she said. They looked at the pictures. The bride wore a suit, hat, and gloves. She looked chic, but Andrea questioned the gloves.

"I think you should wear a hat," Trudy said. "Get one with a large brim."

"I haven't worn a hat for years, but it would be fun."

She confided in Trudy that she had bought a red cocktail dress that she would wear on Saturday.

"Oh, that's so exciting. I'm sure you'll look terrific. Have a picture taken so I can see it."

"I have pictures from New York in my purse. Charles just gave them to me this weekend. I'll go and get them."

Looking at the pictures, Trudy said, "He's so handsome, and he wants to get married, not just shacking up. So many couples do that rather than marry."

"I know." It gave Andrea an idea. Perhaps they could live together. Then there wouldn't be any commitment from Charles if she became ill. He could leave if he wanted to. It was a solution provided Charles would agree to it.

It was Saturday afternoon on the day of the cocktail party. Andrea came home early from work and relaxed in the tub. She felt for the lump. It was difficult to find. Had it gotten so small? Small or big, it was a difficult secret to keep from Charles.

She moisturized her face, neck, arms, and legs. Her arms were still firm, but she should probably exercise to keep them in shape. Would Charles love her if she were fat? He was a little chubby himself, but it didn't hurt at all on his big frame. Why was it that men could gain weight, but not women? She blew-dried her hair, painted her nails red and applied makeup, not much—just a little mascara to bring out her eyes—and blush on her cheeks. Dressed in her fancy underwear, she danced in front of the mirror.

It will be fun to see Charles' reaction. He hasn't seen my red dress either.

She stepped into the dress and wriggled to zip it up.

No matter how much she pulled on the dress, the upper part of her breasts showed. Her high-heeled black shoes made her legs look shapelier, not that there was anything wrong with her legs. Her hose had a pattern. She got her black satin evening clutch out of the closet and moved some necessities from her purse to the bag—a comb, lip-gloss, and a compact.

She had never sat down in the tight dress. Best to try it at home first. The dress scooted up making it look even shorter than before.

I might not be sitting down at the party, but I'll have to in the car.

Panicking, she brought out a black shawl made of lace to take along. She could place it over her legs in the car and if she had to sit down at the party.

Charles was already pulling up in the driveway. He looked smart in a dark suit as he walked toward her door. Soon, he would be ringing the doorbell. She needed a minute to calm her nerves. One last look in the mirror, and she went to open the door for him.

"Oh my, is this lady my date? You look even more beautiful than usual, darling. As Todd would say, you look hot! I love your dress."

"I hope I won't embarrass you."

"Embarrass? All the men will envy me, and all the women will be envious of your dress."

"Is it too short?"

"Definitely not, I love seeing your legs. The farther up the better," he joked. "Seriously, you look good in red, darling."

"That's what the salesclerk said."

He bent down to kiss the top of her breasts. "You look delicious," he said.

Andrea saw in his eyes that he appreciated her new look. He opened the car door for her, and she sat down sideways before swinging her legs inside. It was the only way to get into the car in that dress, and it was the way that queens and princesses did it. She felt like a princess. Before Charles had entered the car from the other side, she had draped her shawl over her thighs that were exposed to what Charles called "the better part."

"No one could guess that you're 53-years old, darling," he said. "Not a day over 50," he joked. Then he broke the big news to her.

"I sold my house. We signed the contract yesterday."

"Really?" Andrea froze, and was glad that Charles concentrated on his driving.

"I need to have the estate sale in the middle of August, and then I have to be out by the first of September. You can set our wedding date, darling."

"Hmm." Andrea stalled. "When is Todd coming home?"

"I'd have to check my calendar on that."

She had avoided answering him, but her biopsy was in a couple of days.

Charles turned into a long driveway to the club. "Well, here we are," he said. "This is where the party is. You're dressed for the occasion, darling."

"This is the country club in Naperville," Andrea said, sounding surprised. "I wasn't paying attention to where we were going."

"You seem a little absent-minded, darling. Is it because of the new dress?"

"I wonder what the other ladies will wear."

"You'll soon find out."

Charles drove all the way up to the entrance where a valet stood ready to park their car. He opened the door for Andrea and she swung her legs and stepped out. Charles was there to take her arm. There was an attendant at the entrance. This must be a fancy affair, Andrea thought. She had been to the club before and never seen such service. Now, she had butterflies in her stomach.

They were ushered into a large room, where Andrea saw several ladies dressed in skimpy cocktail dresses. She was not the only one. Charles looked at her and smiled. His eyes said, *See, I told you so.* That was all she needed to feel assured.

A man approached them saying, "Hello, Charles. Please introduce me to your lovely lady."

"This is my fiancée, Andrea Holm."

"Andrea, this is the judge I told you about, James Dickenson."

"I'm pleased to meet you, Mr. Dickenson."

"My pleasure, Miss Holm. Have you been trying to hide this beauty from us, Charles?"

"Yes, I thought I'd better."

"I'm so pleased you could come. Grab a glass and help yourself to the buffet."

"Charles, what's the occasion for this party?" Andrea asked.

"It's a fundraiser. The agency pledges. My partner is here, also. Oh, there he is with his wife. I want to introduce you."

"Andrea, this is Spencer Brown and his wife, Diana."

"Finally we get to meet your fiancée," Spencer said. He was shorter than Charles, a little pudgy, but very charming.

"Yes, the beautiful lady on my arm is Andrea Holm," Charles said.

Andrea thought about the accident claim that Spencer Brown worked on. He looked at her with curious eyes.

"I trust you've recovered from your accident, Miss Holm," he said.

"I have."

Diana faced her and said, "It was quite an encounter you had with Charles. I'm glad it turned out so well."

"Yes, we're both thankful for that," Andrea said.

"How about some champagne, so we can drink a toast to the happy couple," Spencer said. He waved to a waiter carrying a tray with glasses filled with the bubbly. Charles took one and gave it to Andrea before taking one for himself.

"Congratulations on your engagement," Spencer said. They sipped the chilled champagne.

"I think we should use first names as usual," Charles said.

"Yes, please call me Andrea."

"I'm so glad to finally meet you, Andrea," Diana said. "You can call me Di. I've heard so much about you, all good, of course."

"Charles jokes a lot, so you can't believe everything he says."

Di laughed. "Yes, he has a good sense of humor."

"But he also has good taste in women," Spencer said.

Andrea blushed at his remark. She looked at Diana's dress. It was white with a low neckline. She wore white sandals with high heels and carried a silvery evening bag. Her hair was blond, definitely colored. They were the same height, and Andrea felt comfortable talking with her.

"What is it like to be married to a lawyer?" Andrea asked in a low voice, leaning closer. "I need to know."

"It's great. These fellows don't work much overtime. And it's good they don't have their office downtown."

"Where do you live?"

"Not far from the office. We bought a property with an old house on it, a teardown. Then we built a new home on the lot."

"Was it a big hassle before it was done?"

Di laughed. "Yes, it was trying at times, but we're happy with the results."

The guests gathered at the buffet table and helped themselves to luscious shrimp, meatballs, mushroom caps, crackers, cheese, and lots of veggies and fruit.

Andrea was afraid of spilling on her dress, so she took only veggies, crackers and cheese. The shrimp looked good though. Eating while standing up was difficult, especially while balancing a glass of champagne.

"Let's sit down at a table," Charles said.

Sitting wouldn't be any easier in the tight dress, but the others sat down, so Andrea had to do the same. She put the shawl on her lap and a napkin on top of it.

"You hardly have anything on your plate," Charles said. "Let me get you more food. This is all we'll get, you know."

"Since we're sitting down perhaps I could eat some shrimp," Andrea said.

"The meatballs are good, too. You have to taste them."

Charles came back with a plate of assorted food.

"These are some of the world's most expensive meatballs and shrimp, don't you agree, Spencer?"

"Yes, I'd say so, but it's for a good cause."

Several people came up to Charles to congratulate him. The men thumped him on the shoulders and said something like, "You, lucky dog." Andrea would never remember the names of his friends and colleagues, but she suspected they would remember her.

"Do you need a break Andrea?" Di asked.

"Yes, let's find the lady's room."

"It must be a little intimidating to be introduced all the time," Di said as she escorted Andrea in the right direction.

"Yes, I feel like I'm on display."

"Charles is a well-liked man, and they are checking you out."

"I'm uncomfortable in this dress."

"You look great. I think you made a good impression."

"What was Elaine like?" Andrea asked when they were inside the ladies' room.

"She was different, not as elegant as you. She was a large woman and always dressed in expensive pantsuits."

As they walked back to join the men, she wondered why she hadn't seen any pictures of Elaine at Charles' house. Perhaps they were in the master bedroom.

Finally, people started to leave. Charles asked her if she was ready to go home.

"Yes, I am."

He draped her shawl over her shoulders and cupped her elbow. It felt good to have Charles to herself.

While they waited for their car, Charles said, "I'm sorry you had to go through so many introductions, darling. It must have been daunting."

"Don't expect me to remember everyone. I'm not as good with names as you are."

"There were just too many new people at the same time. You handled it well."

"Why did the men call me Miss Holm?

"That's what we call all young-looking women with no children in tow. It's also safe when we don't know if they are married. Or would you rather be called ma'am?"

"That's what the paramedics called me, so I don't want to be reminded of that. When I saw Spencer, I wondered how the insurance claim is going."

"We're working on it. The kid that hit me claims that the accident was your fault because you slowed down, but he should have retained a safe distance in the bad weather. So I don't think you've to worry about that, honey."

It had never occurred to Andrea that the accident could be her fault, so she didn't worry about it.

"I just want to go home and take off this tight dress," she said.

"I'll be glad to help."

Andrea smiled at the thought of him discovering her red lingerie. She was determined not to think about the outcome of her biopsy.

Chapter 19

Jessica was at Andrea's to tell her about her trip to Copenhagen and Kristian's wedding.

"But first things first, how did the cocktail party go?"

"I graduated into the high-class society of Charles' colleagues and business friends, and he says that I passed with flying colors," Andrea said.

"You mean the color of red?"

"Yes, the dress turned out to be appropriate. The party was at the Naperville Country Club. I met Charles' partner and his wife and also the judge who will marry us."

"Awesome."

"It was. Now I want to hear about your trip and Kristian's wedding."

"I'll start from the beginning," Jessica said. "I boarded a Scandinavian Airlines jet at O'Hare airport for a 10:00 p.m. departure and landed in Copenhagen eight hours later. I slept a little on the plane. At the end of the flight, I could see the approach to Copenhagen. I saw the long bridge to Sweden and the wind turbines out in the water. The grounds were green and lush. I saw lots of red roofs and church steeples. I saw ships and sailboats on the water. It was beautiful.

"Kristian met me at the Kastrup airport and welcomed me to Copenhagen. He asked me what I wanted to see, and I told him the Little Mermaid, the Tivoli Gardens, and the palace. He took me to the Little Mermaid right away. She sits on a rock in the harbor. She's little and she has legs and also a fishtail."

"In the Hans Kristian Andersen's fairytale, it changes between legs and a tail," Andrea said.

"I know. Here're my snapshots and some postcards that show her from the front. She's looking out toward the sea."

"It must have been exciting for you."

"It was, Mom. Wait till you hear this. Kristian drove me across the bridge to Sweden so I could see the country that Nana's parents came from. We only saw a small area across the straight, but it was lovely. I felt a connection with both Sweden and Denmark. Now, I want to ask Nana which part of Sweden her parents came from so I can go there some other time. I can't wait to tell my students what I've seen."

"I can understand that. What does Kristian's fiancée look like?"

"Marie is tall and slim with blond hair and blue eyes. She prepared supper for us at Kristian's place. It was delicious, but then I got tired from the jetlag. I sat in a chair and almost fell asleep. There's a 7-hour time difference. Marie drove me to her apartment and gave me the keys. The apartment was very comfortable, but I only slept there. There was fresh food in the refrigerator and groceries in the pantry.

"The next morning, Marie took me to the Tivoli Gardens. It has 400,000 varieties of flowers. They don't bloom all at the same time, but the roses were in bloom. Mom, it was so incredibly beautiful and the gardens are so large. There're at least 50 restaurants there and we ate in one of them. There's a lot of beautiful art. We went on one ride in the amusement park, but we didn't stay to see any shows. The Tivoli is even more beautiful at night with all the lights. Then we shopped at *Strøget*, the famous street near Tivoli. We also rode bicycles. We had so much fun." Jessica paused to go and get something from her bag.

"Here Mom, I bought you a present." It was a royal-blue T-shirt decorated with small yellow crowns. "The crowns symbolize the union between the three kingdoms, Denmark, Sweden, and Norway, named after a city in Sweden called Kalmar where the agreement was made in 1398. I don't know how long it lasted."

"Thank you so much, Jessica. The shirt is beautiful, but you didn't have to bring me a present."

"The next day, Kristian took me to the castle. We saw the changing of the guard, and it was like watching a movie. The guards wore those tall bearskin hats like they do in England. Queen Margarethe was not in residence, so we could go on a tour of the palace. She was at her summer palace with her family. These postcards show the palace. They're much better than I could take myself. The Danish monarchy is the oldest in Europe and goes back to the year 899. The history is so incredibly old over there. There are four palaces close to each other. The royal family residence is Amalienborg. Here're some pictures of the royals."

Jessica pointed out the members of the royal family and Andrea learned that the queen was the daughter of Princess Ingrid of Sweden and was married to Prince Henrik. Crown Prince Frederik had recently married a commoner, Mary Donaldson. Prince Joachim had been married, but was divorced.

"It sounds like a normal family," Andrea said.

"On the third day, Kristian and Marie took me out in the countryside to where my grandparents Holm were born. It was so exciting. I loved the quaint landscape. We saw farms and homes with beautiful yards and the Danish flag waving in the wind. The weather was warm and sunny, not hot and humid like in Chicago at this time of the year. The air was so fresh and invigorating.

We saw the old schoolhouse that my grandfather had attended. It's not used as a schoolhouse anymore but has been preserved as a museum. The outside was red brick with white trim around the windows. We could go inside and sit at the desks, and we could write our names and addresses in the guest book by the door. After my name, I wrote, 'granddaughter of Felix Holm, who attended this school.' It was awesome. Kristian took us to the church that both of his parents had attended. At one time, Kristian had gone to the pastor's office and seen their names in the ministerial-acts book. He showed us the graves of our ancestors. Here're the pictures."

Andrea studied the inscriptions on the headstones and wanted to know what they meant, and Jessica explained.

"Now I've more of an appreciation for my heritage. It was too bad that my grandparents Holm were killed in an automobile accident in this country. I don't remember much of them."

"Some day, I'll tell you what I know about them."

"We went inside the church and Kristian and Marie met with the minister. They were married in that church two days later?"

"I didn't know that. How appropriate."

"I'll tell you about the wedding in a minute. Now, I want to tell you about the place where my grandfather Holm was born. It was an old stone house built of natural stone. Kristian said that the walls were two feet thick. We couldn't go inside, but here's a picture of the outside."

"Unbelievable. Did you see where your Grandma Holm was born?"

"No, that place had been erased. Her parents were born in Sweden, and now I want to research that part of the family tree. Before we drove back to the city, we stopped at a country pub for lunch. In the evening, we had a drink at Fred's place. Fred is Kristian's best friend. We arrived in three cars, and ours arrived first. A church is a *kirke* in Danish. It was decorated so beautifully with live birch trees and wildflowers. A farmer in the area had cut the trees and brought them in the same morning, and the church smelled wonderful. I've never seen live trees inside a church before."

Andrea could only imagine it all.

"We were surprised when the locals began to arrive. Distant relatives, friends, and neighbors came into the church. They whispered as they signed their names in the guest book and sat down in the back of the church. Marie's parents greeted some of them before sitting down in the front pew. They are from the same area but live in the city."

"Wish I could have been there, but you're describing it so beautifully, Jessica."

"The organ began to play. It was beautiful. When the people in the back rose, I turned around to see Kristian and Marie walking up the aisle arm in arm. They came in together."

"What did Marie wear?"

"She wore an off white, short gown with a wide skirt and tight bodice. She carried a bridal bouquet of wildflowers. Kristian wore a fancy suit and bow tie. They looked surprised, when they saw all the people. Turning left and right, nodding and smiling brightly, they radiated happiness. It was their big day and there were more guests than they had anticipated. The ceremony was in Danish and I tried to follow it in the *salmebok* that was placed before us. I could understand some of it," Jessica said. "In print, Danish looks a little bit like German."

Andrea thought of her planned marriage to Charles. It would be a civil ceremony and nothing like a church wedding, but it was what they both wanted. For Kristian and Marie, it was their first marriage and it should be festive. Andrea looked at Jessica who had stars in her eyes. Perhaps she envisioned a church wedding with Jason.

"Marie's sister, Josephine, was the bridesmaid. She held the bridal bouquet during the ring ceremony. The words were the same as in America, but in Danish. At the end, the minister announced in English, 'May I present to you Mr. and Mrs. Kristian Holm.' Perhaps he was imitating our American custom," Jessica said.

"Outside, the locals threw rice at them and applauded, but stood aside until the closest family had greeted the newlyweds. Then they came forward with outstretched hands. Kristian thanked them all for coming. Fred organized a photo session while the locals looked on. Here're the pictures I got from Fred and some are mine."

Andrea looked at the guests closely and asked who they were. Jessica knew the names of some of the relatives.

"Where was the reception?" Andrea asked.

"It was at Marie's parents' home in the city. We had a wonderful time. Everyone wanted to meet me and talk with me. Their English is very good. We toasted the bridal couple in champagne and then there was all the food. Lots of different kinds of fish and meat served as a buffet."

"Did they have a wedding cake?"

"Yes, but it wasn't as tall as here because they served many kinds of pastries and cookies," Jessica explained.

"Mom, what we call Danish pastries here is called *smørrebröd* in Denmark. It's written with a slash through the o."

"I know, because your father told me."

"The pastries are rich, delicious, and loaded with calories. People eat them between meals with coffee or tea, and I didn't see one overweight person."

"Are they exercising more, you think?"

"They ride bicycles as often they can."

"I'm so glad you could go and experience all this," Andrea said.

"I can't wait to tell my students about it."

To hear about Jessica's trip and Kristian's wedding had taken Andrea's mind off the upcoming biopsy for a little while.

"Now, let's have a cup of tea," Andrea said. "I bought this tin of Danish cookies. I'm sure they're not even close to the real thing, but it says they are made with butter."

Chapter 20

Nana arrived early on the day of the biopsy. Andrea wore a sweat suit to make undressing easy. She gave the direction as Nana drove them to the local hospital.

Once there, Andrea signed the papers, but did not check the place where it said that she would agree to a mastectomy.

"This part comes as a shock to me," she said to the nurse.

The nurse explained that some women preferred to have it done immediately if the lump was malignant.

Despite the local anesthesia, Andrea felt the pressure when the needle was inserted. She could follow the progress on a monitor. When the procedure was over, the technician said, "We'll check this right away."

They wheeled Andrea into another room to wait. Nana joined her. "How was it?" she asked.

"I heard a click and then it was done. They're checking it now. I'm so nervous. It's good to have you here, Nana."

When the doctor came in, he said, "It's negative. We can't see any cancerous cells, but we recommend a mammogram in six months."

"No cancer cells?" Andrea could hardly believe the good news.

"We'll send it to the lab to be confirmed, but we don't think you've anything to worry about. You can go home and enjoy your health."

"Thank God," Nana said as she embraced her daughter. They both had tears in their eyes.

"That's good news. Best of all, I can get married."

"Yes, honey, you can get married."

As soon as the laboratory had confirmed the negative reading of the biopsy, Andrea shared the good news with Charles. It was the first time he learned about her cancer scare. His eyes were full of sympathy for her ordeal. He put his arms around her and asked, "Why didn't you tell me?"

"I didn't want you to worry in case it was nothing, but I told my mother."

"I had no inkling that anything bothered you."

"I was determined to be as happy as I could be, but if it had been cancer that needed treatment, I would have cancelled our wedding."

"Cancelled our wedding! I'm shocked. You mean postpone?"

"No, cancel, for your sake."

"Why?"

"Because you already had a wife with cancer. I don't know if I could've let you go, but you would've had that choice. I love you so much. Perhaps we could have lived together without being married—provided that I got through the treatments all right."

"I would have been your live-in boyfriend?"

"If you still wanted to have me?"

"It would have been better than losing you, darling, but I don't know how you could think that I would leave you. I love you for better or worse, in sickness and health."

"It's reassuring to hear you say that, Charles, and I feel the same way. Whatever life has in store for us, we'll face it together."

Tears rolled down Andrea's cheeks, tears of relief and happiness. Charles kissed them away, and they held each other tightly—as if they would never let go.

"We've lots of plans to make. Our love has been tested, yours more than mine. You're precious to me."

They sat with their arms around each other for a long time thinking about how blessed they were.

"I should call the judge and give him the date for our wedding. He might be busy if we wait too long," Charles said.

Andrea went to fetch a calendar. She had looked at it many times and wondered if they could be married in August. "If it's alright with you, tell him August 20th. I hope it's still available."

"I'll be happy to do that. Todd will be home by then."

"And we should tell everyone that we don't want any gifts."

"We've everything we need and more."

"You can move your leather furniture to my den, honey. It will make you feel more at home."

"I'll always feel at home wherever you are, darling, but I appreciate your offer because I like my den furniture."

"I know you do. If there's anything else you would like to bring, go ahead."

"Perhaps the oriental rug that's in my den. It was a gift from my parents."

"It would look great on the hardwood floor with your furniture."

"I can't wait for Saturday, darling. Wear your red lingerie."

Andrea sat outside and relaxed in the sunshine when Charles called on her cell phone.

"The judge said August 20th will be fine, and if you agree, the ceremony will be at the Drake Hotel. It's much nicer than City Hall, and our families can be present."

"It sounds wonderful, Charles."

"We need to get our wedding license ahead of the time."

"Yes, of course."

"My son Matt said he would be proud to be a witness."

"So August 20th it is." She drew a heart around the date in her calendar, stuck it back on the wall and felt like she was the luckiest woman in the world.

Andrea called her mother to tell her the date and the change in plans. "With the teenagers and children, the dinner might be too expensive for you," she said.

"Don't worry about it. What else should I use my money for? I don't travel any more. It will give me a chance to get the family together and meet your new relatives."

Andrea understood the part about family, because it was so seldom they were all together with Nana.

Andrea called Jessica next. "May I come over?" she asked.

"Of course, Mom. It's Wednesday, so I was expecting you," Jessica said.

When Andrea told her daughter about the cancer scare, Jessica was both surprised and horrified.

"Why didn't you tell me, Mom?"

"In case it was nothing, I didn't want you to worry, and it turned out to be nothing. I feel like I have a new lease on life."

"I'm thankful for that, Mom." Jessica was quiet while taking it all in.

"I'm so sorry you had to go through all that," she continued. "But now we've a wedding to look forward to. Have you decided on the date yet?"

"August 20th."

"Mom, then you might have to count on two more guests."

"Who?"

"Kristian and Marie are arriving that week."

"Great. Of course, they'll be invited. It will be fun to meet Marie."

"What will you wear for your wedding, Mom?"

"What do you think about a wide-brimmed hat?"

"That would be nice. What else?"

"Perhaps a suit?"

"I think we'll have to go to the Oak Brook Mall for that."

"It will have to be on my day off."

"Mom, how long are you going to continue to work?"

"I'll ask for part time after the wedding. And I need vacation time for our trip to Paris."

"You're really going to Paris! You're so lucky, Mom."

"I know, but I think I'm luckier for not having cancer."

"I agree."

"The judge will come to Drake Hotel to marry us. I met him at the cocktail party. After the ceremony, Nana will give a dinner also at Drake. It will be a family celebration."

"I'm looking forward to meeting Charles' family."

Andrea told Jessica that Charles had sold his house and that he would move in with her. "We haven't found another house that we like."

"I kind of like the idea of my childhood home still being in the family."

"Maybe one day, you and Jason can have it. Charles and I might buy another one after awhile."

Chapter 21

While working at the bookstore, Andrea told Bob that she wished to go down to part time after her marriage and that she would take her vacation two weeks following the wedding.

"Trudy knows someone who's willing to work part time," she said.

"Are you sure you'll continue to work at all after your marriage?" Bob asked.

"As long as I don't have to work on weekends."

"I can't promise that."

"If it comes to working on weekends, I will resign."

"I'd hate to see you go," Bob said, "but free weekends?"

Andrea understood that her request was a deal-breaker, but she was willing to take the risk.

Charles had arranged a family gathering at his place. Matt and Cindy, and Linda and Ed were there when Andrea arrived. Matt looked like Todd, only more mature. Cindy wore her natural blond hair pulled back in a ponytail. Cindy and Linda were busy packing china and crystal, and Andrea offered to help. Charles provided the cartons and the packing material.

Matt and Cindy had rented a van so they could take home the antique furniture they had selected. Linda and

Ed said they would come back for theirs. When the van was loaded, they all had a barbeque on the patio.

On Sunday evening, Charles sounded upset when he called. Andrea listened carefully to what he said.

"When I came to the airport to pick up Todd, I thought that Carl was with him. Instead, he pushed the luggage for a girl I had never seen before. At first, I thought he had met her on the plane and just helped her with her luggage, but he introduced her and said that she was coming home with us. He usually sits up front with me, but he scooted into the backseat and sat beside her. When I tried to make light of it by saying it was funny that Carl had turned into a girl, Todd just said that Carl had decided to stay longer."

"So it's a girlfriend then?" Andrea said.

"So it appears."

"Maybe she's just here for a visit?"

"I asked Todd what his plans were, but he was evasive. Perhaps you could talk to Erin and find out more. Can you come tonight, darling? I'll put hamburgers on the grill."

"I'm coming, Charles. It sounds like you need some female help."

"Thanks, I do."

Todd and the girl sat on the patio when Andrea arrived. Todd rose and said, "This is Erin O'Brian. We met in Ireland." Erin had red hair and wore no makeup. She looked pale. Maybe she was tired from the trip.

Lilly Setterdahl

Andrea pressed the girl's hand, and said, "Pleased to meet you, Erin. Is this your first time in the States?"

"Yes."

"How long are you planning to stay?"

"I don't know. My visa is for three months." She spoke with an Irish accent.

"And you, Todd, you'll start your university classes soon?"

"Yes," he said. "Dad has rented an apartment for us."

"Us?"

"Well, it was for me, but I'll take Erin with me."

"But her visa is only good for three months."

"She can enroll in classes and get a student visa."

"That's news to me," Charles said. He stood by the door and heard what Todd said.

"I'm sorry I didn't tell you, Dad."

Charles looked shocked. He turned to Erin and asked, "How old are you?"

"18."

"At least you're of age in this country. When is your birthday?"

"It was in March."

"Have you graduated from high school?"

"Yes, I graduated in June."

"Erin would like to attend college here," Todd said.

"Have you met her parents, Todd?"

"Yes, I have."

Charles looked back at Erin, and asked, "Are your parents alright with you coming here?"

Erin looked down. "They didn't exactly like that I left like this," she said.

"I can imagine. Did they pay for your ticket?"

"No, Todd did." Erin's face had turned red.

"That was something else I meant to tell you, Dad. I charged it."

Andrea noticed that Charles tried hard to stay calm. His cheek muscles twitched.

"Would you help me in the kitchen?" he asked Andrea.

"Yes, of course." They closed the door.

"What should I do?" Charles looked bewildered.

"I think you have to go with the flow. If you show anger, they'll only dig in deeper"

"I hope to God she isn't pregnant."

"For heaven's sake, Charles. I think your son is smarter than that."

"How can they be so sure about each other so soon?"

"Well, we'd only known each other a short time before we were in love."

"That's true, but it's different."

"Yes, the distance between them for one thing. Todd didn't want to leave her behind. Give him some credit for that."

"You sure can put a positive spin on it."

"When can Todd have the apartment?"

"I'm already paying rent for it. Otherwise, it would have rented to someone else. That's how it is in university towns. Now, he has established a residence."

"Is it furnished?"

"No, I promised Todd that he could take the furniture he needed from here."

"Then you should keep that promise. They could go down there now."

"But I don't want Erin to stay here until then. Could she stay with you?" Charles sounded desperate.

"Yes, I'll talk to her," Andrea said. She felt sorry for Charles, who stood in the door opening with the raw hamburgers on a plate. He looked very much like a worried father.

"I'll tell Todd to put these hamburgers on the grill, and we can get the rest ready," he said.

When Charles came back to the kitchen, Andrea was looking in the refrigerator for condiments. She got out the mayo, mustard, and ketchup.

"Do you have any lettuce and tomatoes?" she asked.

"Yes, they are on the counter."

Andrea rinsed the lettuce while Charles sliced the tomatoes.

"I've heated a can of baked beans. Teenagers eat a lot," Charles said.

Andrea stirred the beans, while Charles watched.

"It can be hard to be a parent," she said.

"He's my youngest, and it's especially hard to see him so grownup."

"I know, but it should also be rewarding to see that he's ready to take on grownup responsibilities."

"I think I can face them now," Charles said, "thanks to you, Andrea."

"The burgers are almost ready," Todd said.

"I hope you like hamburgers." Charles said to Erin.

"Yes, I do, sir."

Charles and Andrea brought out the rest of the food. Andrea carried the conversation by talking with Erin and asking her what she would like to study at the university.

"Perhaps Business," Erin said shyly.

When Todd had eaten two hamburgers and a heap of beans, he wiped his mouth, looked at his dad and said, "Dad, I'd like to rent a U-Haul truck and pack the furniture you promised me. I'll take Erin with me down to the apartment and get settled so that she can enroll in classes."

"If you think you can handle the responsibility."

"I can handle it, Dad. I'll get a job. If I come down before the other students, it will be easier to find a job."

"But your classes have to come first."

"Yes, I know, Dad."

"I can get a part-time job also," Erin said. "I don't want to be a burden."

"You won't be able to work until you're enrolled at the university," Andrea said. "I know that because my sister works with exchange students. They can only work on campus, but there're always jobs there at minimum wage."

Todd sent an appreciative look at Andrea. "I promise to come back for your wedding," he said.

"What about your car?" Charles asked Todd.

"I can hang it behind the truck, or come back for it."

"I'd rather see that you come back for it," Charles said.

"Then I'll bring my bike instead. It's easier to get around campus on a bike than with a car," Todd said.

Erin started to stack the dishes. "I'll take these to the kitchen," she said. Andrea followed her with the leftovers.

"Erin," she said. "We need to talk."

"Alright."

"Todd's dad doesn't feel comfortable about you staying here. You can come home with me. I think it would be best until you leave with Todd. I don't live far from here."

"That's a relief. I don't feel comfortable staying here either, and there're some things I need to buy."

"Do you have money?"

"Yes, I have euros."

"We can exchange those for dollars, and I can help you with your shopping."

"I appreciate that so much. I haven't unpacked my suitcase, so we can take it to your car right away."

Todd strolled into the kitchen. "How're you two getting along?" he asked.

"We're getting along just fine," Andrea assured him.

"I'm going home with Mrs. Holm," Erin said.

176

"You are?" Todd sounded surprised.

"Yes, she'll help me with my shopping. You and your dad can rent the truck and pack it. You don't need me for that. I'll stay with Mrs. Holm until we're ready to leave. That's what I want, Todd."

"I'll take your suitcase to her car then."

"It's for the best. I can call my parents and reassure them."

Charles was cleaning the grill when they came outside. Andrea went up to him and said, "Erin is coming home with me." He turned around and whispered in her ear, "Thank you darling."

"Thank you for supper, Mr. Bordeaux," Erin said.

"You're welcome. Andrea will take good care of you." To Andrea, he said, "I'll call you."

Todd went with Erin and Andrea to the car, carrying the suitcase. He hugged Erin. "Take care, sweetie." To Andrea he said, "Thanks again."

In the car, Erin confided to Andrea that she needed tampons and a prescription for birth control pills.

"Yes, that's important. We can buy the tampons today. But I'll have to make an appointment with my doctor for the pills."

"You're so kind. I can't tell you how much I appreciate it."

"I was young once."

"And you're marrying Todd's dad."

"Yes, I am."

Erin said she liked the guestroom at Andrea's house. She opened her suitcase and took out a few things.

"I need to iron my shirts," she said.

"I'll put up the ironing board for you. While you iron, I can get the sheets on the bed," Andrea said.

First thing Monday morning, Andrea dialed her doctor's number and said that she had a young friend who needed birth-control pills and asked how soon they could have an appointment.

"You could bring her Wednesday morning. It's your free day, isn't it?"

"Yes. Her name is Erin O'Brian, but she won't be a regular patient. She's going to U of Illinois. I'll take care of the bill."

"See you both on Wednesday at 9:30," the receptionist said.

Andrea could hear that Erin was in the bathroom, so she set the table for breakfast and made enough coffee for both of them. When Erin came into the kitchen, she wore jeans and a white shirt.

"Good morning, Erin. Did you sleep well?"

"Good morning. I had a good night's sleep, but I hadn't slept at all on the plane. I was so worried about how I would be received. But you've been wonderful, ma'am."

"Please call me Andrea. Would you like coffee or tea?"

"I'd prefer tea, but you've already made coffee."

"No problem. Tea is fast."

"Toast and marmalade?"

"Yes, please."

"I made a doctor's appointment for you at 9:30 on Wednesday."

"Thank you, Andrea. I hope that Todd doesn't want to leave before then."

"I'll tell Charles that he can't. Wednesday is my day off, and that's when we're going shopping after we've been to the doctor. We can go to a mall. Today, I've arranged for you to be with my daughter, Jessica. She's a fourth-grade teacher. Jessica will take you to a bank. I'm working until six; then I'll come and get you."

"I hope it isn't too much trouble?"

"Not at all. Tomorrow, Todd will bring you downtown Chicago."

"Great!" Erin looked happy, and Andrea could tell that going downtown with Todd topped everything.

"Remember to call your parents."

"I've already talked to them on my mobile."

"Good. I'll take you to Jessica's before I go to work."

Chapter 22

When Andrea picked up Erin at Jessica's that evening, she learned that they had been to a daycare center, where a friend of Jessica's worked. Erin had spoken to the children about Ireland.

"The children said it was so-o-o cool to meet someone who had actually grown up in Ireland." Jessica said. "That's something they will remember."

"I taught them an Irish song," Erin said with a pretty smile. It was the first time Andrea had seen her smile.

"What else did you do? Did you go to a bank?"

"Yes, I exchanged my money, and then Jessica drove by a community college and told me that I could take classes there, but I'd rather go with Todd."

"I understand," Andrea said. She didn't think that the two teenagers would change their minds.

"It's so hot and humid here. I'm not used to it. I need to buy shorts," Erin said.

"Yes, it's hot and humid here in the summers. That's what makes the corn grow. It was 102 degrees at O'Hare the other day."

"I don't know how much that's in Celsius, but I've never experienced anything like it."

"It might be close to 40 degrees Celsius, but it was probably cooler by the lake."

"Todd said it gets cold here in the winter?"

"Yes, it gets cold, but it can still be pleasant in the first part of October.

They were sitting on the rust-colored couch in the den when Andrea told Erin that Charles would bring his leather furniture and that she would give the den furniture to charity.

"But yours are still good." Erin jumped up and pointed to the couch and the chairs. Erin's comment gave Andrea an idea.

"If you like my furniture, you and Todd can have them for your apartment," she said.

"That would be wonderful. They would be perfect for us," she said. "I was afraid that Todd would bring fancy furniture from his home." She excused herself and went to her room to call Todd.

Erin's excitement reminded Andrea of when she and Philip had started out with second-hand furniture. After Erin had gone to bed, she called Charles and told him everything she had planned for Erin and her day with Jessica.

"I don't know what I'd do without you."

"How're things going at your end?"

"Todd told me that you'd like to give them your den furniture."

"Yes, Erin accepts the offer, and it sounds like Todd does, too. What's Todd doing?"

"He's fixing Linda's old bike for Erin. On Wednesday, we'll pick up the U-Haul. Could we bring my leather furniture then and pack yours?"

"Yes, of course. We'll try to be home early from the mall."

"Don't rush. It will take time for us to load the furniture here. Should I bring the lamps from my den also?"

"Go ahead and bring them," Andrea said.

"Linda and Ed would like to meet Erin. Ed was the one who told Todd not to come home with an Irish girl, and now he's curious about her. Linda said she would give them some kitchen supplies. They can take some from here also."

"Don't forget to pack sheets and towels. The more they take with them, the less they have to buy."

"Thanks for the reminder. I can't wait to see you again. I miss you."

"I miss you, too. Saturday night is coming up. On Sunday, I don't have to be at work until one o'clock."

"Can't wait."

On Tuesday, Todd came to take Erin to downtown Chicago. Andrea drove them to the train station. When Erin came back to Andrea's, she bubbled with enthusiasm.

"The Museum of Science and Industry is a great place and we saw only a small part of it."

"Yes, I know it's big. I'm glad you went there."

"We also went to Millennium Park. I took pictures of the Bean."

"Charles and I went there earlier this year. It's a fun place, isn't it?"

182

"Fun and educational, I think Chicago is fantastic. We went to the top of Sear's Tower and saw Lake Michigan and the city in three directions. Todd pointed out some of the many towns. There're so many of them. I got a better idea of how large the metropolitan area really is."

"Yes, nearly ten million people live in the greater Chicago area."

"And there's so much traffic everywhere."

"Yes, especially in the morning and at night when everyone goes to and from work."

"I think I should get a book about Chicago," Erin said.

"There're some in my bookcase. I'll show them to you."

Erin selected a book and then spent most of the evening looking at the pictures and reading about Chicago.

On Wednesday morning, Andrea sat in the waiting room while Erin saw the doctor. Erin smiled when she came out with a prescription in her hand.

"Your doctor is very nice, Andrea," she said. Erin put the prescription in her purse and took out her wallet.

"Where do I pay?"

"You don't. I took care of it. It's easier that way."

"Really? Thank you so much."

"You'll have to buy health insurance if you're staying."

"Oh, really? I didn't know that."

Out in the car, Erin told Andrea that the nurse had checked her heart and lungs and asked many questions.

"They had to make sure you were healthy before prescribing the pills."

"The doctor said it takes a while before the pills work. I didn't know that. I can buy the pills with this prescription downstate, but I'd like to buy some now."

"Yes, we'll stop at the drugstore."

Andrea had planned to buy a wedding outfit together with Jessica that day, but it had to wait. While Erin looked at clothes for herself, Andrea checked what was available for her, and tried on a few hats. Erin bought a pair of shorts and paid for them with her new dollar bills.

"Is there anything else you're interested in?" Andrea asked.

"I don't want to spend more money. Todd says I have to pay tuition for my classes, and I don't know how much that would be."

"I don't know either. Let's get some lunch before we go home."

While waiting for their food Andrea said, "There's something else you should know. I don't think you can live off campus. Foreign students usually have to live in a dorm."

"Todd mentioned that to me."

"What does your dad do for a living?"

"He's a detective for the Dublin Police Department, and my mum is a hospital nurse."

"Do you have younger siblings?"

"Yes, I have two younger brothers, but they won't be in college for several years. My parents should be able to help me with the cost of tuition. I hope everything works out. I love Todd," Erin said.

"I understand, but you're both very young and your feelings might change. Boys are not as mature as girls at your age."

"I know that, but Todd seems to be more mature than other boys his age."

"He's a good young man. He probably takes after his father."

"I've a lot of respect for Mr. Bordeaux."

"It took him awhile to get over the shock of seeing you with Todd at the airport, and he had to make sure that your stay here is legal."

"I understand."

"How did you two meet?"

"We met at a disco. Todd asked me to dance and then we saw each other almost every day."

"So Todd didn't get much hiking done after that, I suppose?"

Erin blushed, but didn't say anything.

"Was Carl with him when you met?"

"Yes, he dated a friend of mine, and I think they like each other."

"You'll meet Todd's sister, Linda, and her husband Ed tomorrow. Linda is an author."

"Wow!"

"Ed sells real-estate. He's of Irish ancestry. We've a lot of Irish people in Chicago. We celebrate St. Patrick's Day by coloring the Chicago River green."

"Amazing. How do they do that? A whole river?"

"It's only temporary, for one day."

"It's been so good of you to spend your free day with me."

"I enjoyed it. Are we ready to go home then?"

"Yes, I'm ready."

"We'd better be home before our guys come."

"You are so cool, Andrea."

It was hot outside and Andrea said it was important to drink a lot of water. She brought a pitcher of lemonade to the den and invited Erin to join her. Erin looked at the TV set and said, "I wonder if we can get BBC here?"

"Yes, we get BBC on one channel. Are you getting homesick?"

"No, it's just that it would be nice to hear some news from home."

"I can understand that. You can also get it on the Internet."

"I know because Todd read the *Chicago Tribune* on the Internet in Ireland."

"Isn't that fantastic? I'm sure that Todd will bring a computer."

"Yes, he said that he has a laptop. E-mail will make it easy to communicate with my family."

Andrea said she had to remove some things from the end tables before they put them in the truck. She carried the framed pictures and knickknacks to the living room.

In the drawers, there were old magazines, and odds-and-ends to clear out.

"Do you want these pillows, Erin?"

"If you don't need them?"

"I don't need them. You can take the lamps also. Charles is bringing his."

"Todd said that his apartment has one bedroom, a living room, and a kitchen."

"I wonder if Charles has any kitchen furniture to spare. Otherwise, there's a set in the basement. I'll show you." Erin rose quickly and followed Andrea to the basement.

"It's an old one with metal legs, but I think they're coming back in style."

"Oh, that's cool. I'll see what Todd says. I don't know how much room there will be on the truck."

When the U-Haul truck drove up in front of her house, Andrea said, "My neighbors will think I'm moving." Charles and Todd unloaded the leather couch wrapped in the rug and put it down in the driveway.

"We need to bring your furniture outside before we can bring anything in," Charles said to Andrea.

"Have you packed a kitchen set yet?" she asked.

"No, mine was too big for them."

"I have an old set in the basement." Turning to Erin, she said, "Why don't you show Todd?"

The two disappeared and Andrea guessed they took the opportunity to kiss.

Todd and Erin came up the stairs carrying the kitchen table. "This is great," Todd said. "It must be old."

"Yes, it's from the Middle Ages, or at least from the 50s," Andrea said. "I got it from my parents a long time ago."

Erin led Todd to the den, and Andrea heard Erin say that they could take everything except the TV set and the bookcase. Erin walked out carrying the pillows, while Todd called on his dad to help him carry the couch. With the work finished, it was time for a break, and Andrea served cold drinks.

"I'd like to clean the floor before you bring in the other furniture," Andrea said.

"I can do that if you give me a mop," Erin said.

"Alright." Andrea took a pail and a mop out of a closet.

Erin was done in a few minutes. "Now, the floor needs to dry before you put the rug on," she said.

"That girl knows what's she's doing," Andrea said.

"My mum taught me those things."

Todd looked proud.

"We can get the chairs from the basement while we're waiting," he said. Erin leapt to his side.

Andrea was amazed how nice Charles' furniture looked in the den.

"Now, I have my own room here," he said. "I can come back whenever I want."

"Let's go home, Dad, we still have boxes of books and other stuff to load tonight."

"All right, you slave-driver," Charles muttered.

"I'll bring Erin over in the morning," Andrea said as they waved goodbye.

When Andrea and Erin arrived at Charles' house on Thursday morning, Charles and Todd were waiting for them outside by the truck. Erin was comfortably dressed in her new shorts. Andrea wished she could stay to see the young people off, but she had to say goodbye to them and go to work. Todd looked at Andrea saying, "Thanks for the furniture and for taking care of Erin." Erin hugged Andrea and thanked her for everything.

"Have a good trip and good luck, you two," Andrea said. "When are you leaving?"

"As soon as Linda and Ed have been here," Todd said.

Charles walked Andrea to her car and gave her a quick kiss.

"Do you feel better now about the kids?" she asked.

"Yes, I've accepted the situation. See you Saturday. I'll bring takeout. Thanks again for your help."

She waved to the trio as she drove away. At the end of the driveway, she met the car with Ed at the wheel and Linda by his side. They rolled down their windows and exchanged a few words before Andrea turned onto the highway.

Chapter 23

Charles and Andrea sat in the den and enjoyed its new look. The heat was oppressive outside, but they were comfortable in the air-conditioned house. They had much to talk about, and most of it concerned Todd and Erin. The kids had arrived safely in Urbana on Thursday and had moved into the apartment. The first thing they had to buy was a window air-conditioning unit, which Charles had promised to pay for. According to the news, people were dying from the heat in some states.

Charles had his arms around Andrea.

"In a way, I feel that we are aiding and abetting them to shack up," he said.

"Times have changed. Jessica lives with Jason. Once Erin is enrolled in classes, I think she'll have to move to a dorm."

"I hope so. Todd is too young to have a live-in girl-friend."

"You don't want them to marry either because it might not last. If they grow apart, it's best that they aren't married."

"As always, you are right my darling." He whistled to prove his point.

"I like Erin. She has a good head on her shoulders, and she made sure she had a prescription for birth control pills."

"Thanks to you, she got it. I told Todd to pack condoms, but he shrugged it off, saying he had everything under control. He also said that since I was going to remarry and sell our home, he wanted to establish his own."

"So he has some leverage on you."

"I can see his point."

"I think they're in love," Andrea said.

"Well, At least infatuated, but they'll have their share of arguments, I'm sure. It still hard to accept that my son would do something so drastic. I suspect that he had already met Erin when I talked to him on the phone and was making plans."

"You're probably right. I know how you feel, Charles, because I didn't like it when Jessica moved in with Jason, but it was nothing I could do about it. They were old enough to make their own decisions."

"But Todd and Erin are too young. I wonder if they will stay together through four years of college."

"You never know. Perhaps we'll get to go to a wedding in Ireland."

"Now, let's not get ahead of ourselves, darling. We have our own wedding to arrange. Todd will come for that, he said, and pick up his car at the same time. Linda and Ed invited him to stay with them, and Erin, too, if she likes to come."

Andrea shifted her position and put her head on Charles' lap while resting her legs on the couch. Charles stroked her legs. "That's nice of them," she said.

"I'm going to put some things in storage. Todd cannot accept his part of the family heirlooms at this time. He only took an old trunk for now and his bedroom furniture," Charles said.

Andrea sighed. "Our wedding is three weeks from now, and I haven't bought my dress yet. I must do it this week."

"You've been busy with Erin." He bent down to kiss her while stroking the inside of her thighs.

"I can't think when you do that," she said, gently moving his hand.

"We have something else we should discus. Did your boss agree to part-time work for you after we're married?" he asked.

"Yes, but he can't guarantee that I won't have to work on weekends." She still felt the vibrations from Charles' touch.

"I'd be lonely without you."

"Well, I told Bob that I'll resign if I have to work weekends."

"The quitting part is alright with me, darling. We can find something else for you to do."

"Like what?"

"I'd have to think about it. Perhaps you could do volunteer work?"

"Do you have anything special in mind?" Andrea sat up.

"It depends on what you're interested in. There're many organizations that depend on volunteers."

"I've given some thought to applying for the position of teacher's aide at Jessica's school."

"It sounds like a good idea."

"Helping children learn to read would be rewarding."

"You'd have summers and holidays off."

Charles rocked Andrea in his arms. That's where she wanted to be. She would prove it to him, time, and time again. It was more important than any job.

He looked at the wall clock and became unusually serious.

"We should make a few things clear from the beginning about who's paying for what after we're married," he said. "You'll get a new charge card and a checking account and I'll pay for your purchases, including groceries."

"That's very generous of you, Charles. I won't be extravagant."

"I think you should continue to own your home. I'll draw up new wills for both of us so that our children are protected."

"You know more about those things than I do, and I trust you."

"Can we do something pleasurable now?" His eyes filled with tenderness as she nestled in his arms. "I've been looking at the wall clock all evening waiting for bedtime," he said.

Andrea and Jessica were at the Oak Brook Mall, searching for something suitable for both of them to wear for the wedding.

"And you need outfits for Paris, Mom," Jessica said.

"Well, I do have clothes in my closet. I don't have to buy everything."

"Of course, you should take your red dress with you to Paris. You can wear your blue dress to any pre-wedding parties. On the plane, you can wear slacks. It's the most comfortable."

"But what should I be married in? That's what we're here for."

Jessica browsed the racks at the large department store.

"Here's a suit in your size, Mom," she said. "It's peach. I think that would be a good color on you."

"All right, I'll try it on. Can you find a hat to go with that?"

Jessica came back with two hats, one off-white and one white. Andrea already had the suit on.

"It fits you, Mom. Now try this hat."

The brim had a lace pattern that filtered the light. Andrea had to admit that the look was appealing. "What about the other one?" She tried the white hat and it looked good as well.

"Now, I don't know which one is the best. Perhaps I'm too short for a wide-brimmed hat."

She looked at the peach suit she had on and said that she didn't like the short sleeves.

"I'd like to look at dresses as an alternative. There's no reason why I can't wear a dress, is there?"

"No reason. I prefer a dress myself."

"I want you to select one, and I'll pay for it." A sales-clerk came forward and asked if they needed help. After about two hours, they were loaded down with shopping bags and looked for a place to eat.

Seated at a table, mother and daughter studied the menu and decided on a salad.

"Next year, we may shop for your wedding, honey," Andrea said.

"If we have a church wedding, I hope that Uncle Kristian will walk me down the aisle."

"I think he'd be honored to take the place of your dad."

They finished their lunch, picked up their shopping bags and walked to Andrea's car.

"I suppose you'll get a new car when you're married to Charles. A Cadillac or something like that?" Jessica said.

Chapter 24

Andrea's cell phone rang while she was on her way to work. Who could it be? Before she could answer, the call had gone to voice mail. The message made her go pale. Her mother was in the hospital. "Please call us back," the voice said. Andrea pulled to the side of the road. Her hands shook as she clicked on reply and got hold of the person who had called.

"Your mother is being examined right now. She has chest pains."

"Oh, my God, it's such a shock."

"She hasn't mentioned chest pains to you?"

"No, she's been active as usual. She was here not long ago. How is she?" Andrea held her breath as she waited for the answer.

"She's resting comfortably for now, but she might need you."

"I'll come as soon as I can, or one of my sisters will come."

Nana was seriously ill. It was the last thing Andrea had expected. Occupied with her own life, she had paid no attention to her mother's health. Is this my punishment for being selfish?

Dear God, don't let Nana die.

Andrea called Kathy. She was at the golf course and was as shocked as Andrea had been. "I'll leave as soon as

I can, she said. "I'll call and ask Nancy if she can come with me. How did Nana get to the hospital?"

"She went in an ambulance."

"Poor Nana."

"I'm on my way to work, but I hope to get off early," Andrea said.

"Keep me informed. I'm on my way to my car. I need to go home and get some things," Kathy said.

Andrea had to work for at least a couple of hours until someone could take her place. She put her phone on vibrate and kept it nearby. Her hands were still unsteady when she opened the cash register. She had a hard time concentrating on her work. During lunch hour, she called the hospital and inquired about her mother's condition.

"The blood test shows that she has suffered a heart attack. We still don't know how extensive. A specialist is examining her now. Your mother is aware of the situation and she has given her consent to treatment."

Heart attack, the words kept ringing in Andrea's ears.

"My sister Kathy is on her way, and I'm coming tonight."

Andrea called Charles and explained why she couldn't see him during the upcoming weekend.

"I'm so sorry about your mother," he said. "It's hard to believe."

"I know. I'm leaving soon and I don't know how long I'll be gone."

"I understand, honey. Drive carefully, and call me when you get there."

"I will." Andrea's voice broke while they exchanged their love sentiments.

She forgot to eat lunch. Bob had to remind her. "I'll go and get something for you," he said.

"Thanks Bob. I think I need a milkshake for energy."

While driving west on the interstate, Andrea thought of how she and Charles had met after the accident. It still amazed her how she could be both unlucky and lucky at the same time. Charles had changed her life. She was the happiest she had been in years. Would Nana's illness prevent her from getting married to Charles as planned? She quickly put the thought aside. For now, nothing was more important than Nana's life.

She was thankful for her transponder that allowed her to pass quickly through yet another toll plaza at DeKalb. She had been at the hospital in DeKalb after her accident. She could see the tall campus buildings of Northern Illinois University. That's where she had gone to college. Where had all the years gone? Now, she looked forward to her future with Charles. They would enjoy life to the fullest. It was so fragile.

Tonight she would sleep in her childhood home in Rockville. Kathy would be with her, unless they had to sit with Nana in the hospital. Kathy hadn't called and it was a concern to Andrea. When Andrea had tried to call her, she didn't pick up.

She drove directly to the hospital and parked. Once inside, she went to the information desk. On the way to

Nana's room, she spotted Kathy with a cell phone to her ear.

"Oh, there you are, Andrea. I was just going to call you."

"How's Nana?" The two sisters fell in each other's arms.

"She has had an angiogram and is resting."

"An angiogram, what's that?"

"As I understand it, they went into her arteries with a scope and opened up a blockage. It's not a risk-free procedure. The patient could die, but Nana had signed the papers herself."

"Poor Nana. Were you here before she went to surgery?"

"Yes, I had just arrived, and I talked to her. She said you should go ahead with the wedding, regardless of what happens to her."

Andrea's eyes burned with tears.

"She's sleeping now."

"I'd like to see her."

The two sisters stood by Nana's bed and thought about the same thing. They could've lost their mother. Their father had been gone for many years. Was she lonely? She had lived alone for 20 years. She played bridge with her friends and she was active in her church, but was it enough? They should have moved her closer to Chicago.

"I should have visited her more often?" Kathy said. "Why didn't I? If I could only do it over."

Nana stirred and opened her eyes. She seemed to have difficulty focusing. Her mouth was dry and her voice hoarse as she tried to speak.

"Kathy," she said.

"Yes, Nana, I'm here, and so is Andrea."

"How're you feeling?" Andrea patted Nana's arm.

"I'm groggy."

"Yes, but you had a procedure that will make you feel better."

"So I survived."

"Yes, we're so thankful for that," Andrea said.

The nurse told Andrea and Kathy that their mother would sleep through the night and that there was no reason for them to stay.

"Alright, we'll go to her house and you can reach us on her phone or on my cell phone. We'll be back in the morning," Andrea said.

"Do you have Nana's house key?" Kathy asked Andrea.

"Yes, I do."

"She doesn't have an alarm, does she?"

"No, they don't need alarms here."

They went to say goodnight to Nana, but she was asleep, so they left the hospital.

Andrea turned onto the tree-shaded street where Nana lived. Kathy was right behind her. They parked in the driveway, and walked to the back door.

"The roses are beautiful," Kathy said.

"Yes, she takes care of her flowerbeds herself, but she hires someone to mow the lawn."

They let themselves into the small, white house with horizontal siding. Everything was neat and tidy except the unmade bed.

"Kathy, did she tell you where she was when she first felt the chest pains?" Andrea asked.

"She told the doctor she was just getting up when the pain started. She chewed an aspirin and sat down on her bed. Her phone was on her night table, so when the pain didn't go away, she called 911. She was told to unlock the front door, grab her purse, and lay down inside the door. She must have passed out, because she couldn't remember anything until she was in the ambulance."

"She had the sense to do all that. It probably saved her life."

"That's what the doctor said."

"When do we get the results of the angiogram?"

"Tomorrow, and if there's extensive damage, she might need heart surgery."

"That's so scary. I want to call Charles."

"Go ahead. I'll find something for us to eat."

When Charles answered, she told him about her mother's condition.

"How's the hospital there? I'm asking in case your mother should need more surgery."

"It's small compared to DeKalb and the Chicago hospitals."

"If her doctor approves, perhaps she could be moved to a bigger hospital near you."

"We'll consider it if we have to. Kathy and I are at Nana's house. We'll sleep in our old girls' room tonight."

"Sleep tight. I miss you, and I love you. I hope your mother will be all right."

Talking with Charles gave Andrea her appetite back. She was actually hungry when she sat down to eat what Kathy had set on the table.

Chapter 25

As Andrea and Kathy were ready to drive to the hospital in the morning, the next-door neighbor, Mrs. Berg, came outside, saying that she had seen the ambulance and asked if she could be of help.

"It's very kind of you Mrs. Berg," Andrea said, explaining what had transpired. "We'll know more later today."

Mrs. Berg was Swedish and she and Nana were good friends. They had been neighbors for a long time.

At the hospital, Andrea and Kathy stood by their mother's bed and listened to what the doctor had to say.

"Unfortunately, you need more surgery, Mrs. Chester," he said. "We need to do a coronary bypass."

Kathy and Andrea were stunned into silence.

"What are my chances, doctor?" Nana asked.

"As with all surgeries there are risks, but you're healthy otherwise, so I believe you can benefit from the surgery. We'll take a blood vessel from your leg and use it for the bypass."

Andrea thought of Charles' advice. "Can the surgery be done at this hospital?" she asked in a shaky voice.

"I recommend Mt. Sinai in Chicago," the doctor said.

"My daughters all live in the Chicago area," Nana said.

"That's another reason to move you then."

"When could she be moved?" Kathy asked.

"As soon as I can get her admitted to Mt. Sinai, and it could be as soon as today."

"Would she have to go in an ambulance?" Andrea asked.

"That's what I recommend in case she needs oxygen."

"Is that alright with you, Nana?" Andrea asked.

"Yes."

"Then I'll issue an order for the transfer. You'll be in good hands, Mrs. Chester."

Kathy and Andrea looked at each other and then grabbed Nana's hands. They both assured her that she would be fine and that they would visit her often.

"I'll miss your wedding, Andrea, but you should still have the dinner as planned."

"Charles and I have planned to go to Paris on our honeymoon, and I'll be worrying about you."

"I don't want you to worry. You should enjoy your honeymoon. Your sisters will look after me."

Nancy was getting ready to come when she received the call. She was bringing her girls, she said.

"You don't have to come, Nancy. We're moving Nana to Mt. Sinai in Chicago. You can visit her there," Kathy said.

"Well then, may I talk to her?"

"Nancy wants to talk to you, Nana."

"Yes, give me the phone."

"Don't cry, Nancy," Nana said. "I'll be alright."

Andrea went out in the corridor to call Charles and tell him about the doctor's recommendation. "I'll probably be home today," she said, "but then we've to face Nana's surgery next week."

"I'll be there for you, darling." It was a great comfort to Andrea.

Kathy and Andrea rang Mrs. Berg's door and told her that their mother would be moved to Chicago for heart surgery. Mrs. Berg told them not to worry about the house. She would look after it and water the flowers, inside and out. She already had the key.

"Please greet your mother from me. I hope the surgery is successful," Mrs. Berg said.

"We'll tell her. She'll be glad to know that you're looking after her house."

"What should I do with her mail?" Mrs. Berg asked.

"I'll go to the post office and forward the mail to my address," Kathy said.

Many thoughts went through Andrea's mind as she packed her mother's clothes, and took the used linen with her. Nana had a strong faith. If she was to depart from this earth, she was ready.

They all sat and waited for the outcome of Nana's surgery while mindlessly leafing through some magazines. Andrea was thinking that no one likes hospitals, but that they are good to have when you need them. She imagined the surgeon cracking open her mother's chest. It was too gruesome for comfort, and it would cause Nana great pain for a long time. Would she ever be able to live alone in her house again? Would she be able to drive the distance from Rockville to Naperville? It would be difficult to part with their childhood home, but they had to face reality. Somehow, Andrea knew that they all prayed for Nana.

Finally, the surgeon, dressed in his green shirt and pants, walked into the waiting room. The three sisters looked at him with eyes filled with anxiety.

"We did the bypass, and it's functioning properly. She'll feel much better and stronger when she gets over the initial discomfort. She's in recovery now. I suggest that you go and get something to eat. When you come back you can come and see your mother for a few minutes."

That night Andrea rested in Charles arms at his house. They talked about death and dying. For the first time, they shared the pain that they had felt when their spouses suffered from their illnesses and died.

"Philip had prostate cancer and it robbed him of his manhood. I knew something was wrong, but he still didn't want to go and see a doctor. He was taking blood-pressure medication, and it can make men impotent.

"Then one evening he got a terrible pain in his kidneys. I drove him to the hospital. We thought he suffered from kidney stones, but there were no stones. Instead, they found an enlarged prostate. The biopsy came out positive for cancer. A body scan showed that the cancer had spread to the bones. It was terminal. The urologist gave him two years to live. At that point, we thought two years was a gift. Philip got medication that kept his PSA in check. He wanted to continue working as long as possible. I took a leave of absence from my job to travel with him in his work. Driving used to be easy for him, but I had to take over most of it as he tired easily. He didn't want me to talk about his cancer, so I had to carry it inside the whole time. I knew I would lose him, and he knew he would die.

"We talked about religion and what I would do after he was gone. He arranged for his funeral. The doctors said that experimental treatment might help. I pushed him in a wheelchair in the corridors of the Northwestern Hospital, but it was too late for experimentation. His PSA was too high. He couldn't stomach the painkillers they gave him, so he relied on over-the-counter pills. He had many sleepless nights. The only hope left was chemo. It would give him six additional months to live. We grasped at straws.

"The chemo was awful, and he got terribly sick. After two treatments, he refused them. His blood count went down and he had to have transfusions. He stayed one night in the hospital, and then he wanted to come home. He said he wished to die at home. I got a hospital bed for him, and cared for him, night and day. I don't know how I got the strength. During his final hours, a nurse came and gave him morphine. He had no fight left in him. Still, it was very hard to lose him."

Andrea hid her tears against Charles' chest.

"Honey, I admire you for taking care of your husband."

"After the funeral, I felt empty. It was so final. There was no way back, but I felt that his spirit was still with me. For six months, it felt like he walked by my side."

"I felt a tremendous guilt for not having been by Elaine's side during her suffering," Charles said. "Linda took her to the chemo treatments and stayed with her while she vomited. Elaine wanted me to sleep in another room. She told me I needed my sleep because I had to work.

"My work kept me away from her. I was at the hospital when she had her mastectomy, and I told her that nothing would change between us, but it did. Her bedroom door remained closed. In the end, she died at the hospital. I was there, but I didn't have to care for her. I feel I came up short, especially compared to you, my dear, dear Andrea."

"I want you to go and have your PSA checked, Charles. If prostate cancer is caught in the early stages, it doesn't have to be fatal."

"Yes, I will. You've already had a breast-cancer scare, so I know you will get your annual mammograms. But you have to promise me not to shut me out like Elaine did if something happens to you."

"I promise." They were both subdued. It was the first night they spent together that they didn't make love, although they made up for it in the morning.

Andrea cut roses from Charles flowerbeds, and located a vase for them. She held it in her lap while Charles drove to the hospital.

Nana was on pain medication, but she was glad to see them.

"I hope the wedding is on," she said.

"The wedding is on," Andrea assured her.

"Here're some roses for you from Charles's flowerbeds."

"They're beautiful. Put them in the window so I can see them."

As they drove home to Naperville, Charles said, "So there's no reason why we shouldn't get our marriage license on Wednesday?"

"Not anymore, but I want to go and see Nana on our way home."

"Of course, I'll come with you to see Nana. I've taken the whole day off. I'll see you Wednesday morning, darling."

Chapter 26

Andrea looked in her mailbox and was happy to find a handwritten envelope from Erin. She couldn't wait to read it, so she tore it open. Erin wrote:

Todd and I like our apartment. Your furniture looks great and so does the furniture from Todd's home. I have registered for the fall semester and plan to major in business.

Todd works fulltime at a car-leasing company. When classes start, it will be part time. I have obtained a social security number so I'm allowed to work on campus. For now, I assist in the admissions office. Later, it might be the cafeteria. I have applied for a student visa, and I hope to get it before my temporary visa expires.

Todd plans to come to your wedding. I'll remain here, but I wish you the very best. I appreciated what you did for me when I arrived as the bewildered girlfriend. Thank you so much for everything. Please greet Jessica and Kathy and thank them for what they did for me. Kind regards, Erin."

P.S. When classes start, I'm moving to a dorm.

The card impressed Andrea. It came a little late, but Erin probably wanted to settle down before writing. She had volunteered to stay behind when Todd was coming to the wedding. Andrea guessed that she didn't have a dress for the occasion.

Charles came at nine o'clock sharp as promised. This time, he brought his winter clothes and boots.

"Could I hang these in your basement, darling?" he asked.

"You can put the winter clothes in the guestroom closet for now—that's what I do with mine—but the boots can go in the basement," she said.

Andrea told him about the card from Erin and let him read it.

"I like the part about her moving into a dorm," he said.

"It will be for the best. She and Todd can still date."

"She might not want to come to our wedding because she's afraid of me," Charles said with a wry smile.

"She told me she has great respect for you, but I suspect she didn't bring a suitable dress. She probably didn't think she would need one."

"I'll talk to Todd about it."

"You could give Todd the money for a dress," Andrea suggested.

"I'll do that, and I'll tell Todd to bring her. How much would she need?"

"I think fifty dollars should do it."

In the car, Andrea said, "I've also been thinking about what we should plan for Thanksgiving and Christmas."

"You think ahead, don't you, darling."

"Yes. Where did you celebrate the holidays last year, Charles?"

"I went to Matt's and Cindy's, but before Elaine became ill, everybody came to our house. Linda and Ed usually go to his parents' house."

"What would you think about having Christmas at our house this year?"

"I'd like that."

"Todd and Erin could come up for their Christmas break. We could invite Matt, Cindy, and their children. Nana would be here, of course." Andrea's eyes glowed with excitement.

"It's always fun to be with the children at Christmas, but what about Thanksgiving?"

"In our family, it's usually at Kathy's."

They talked some more about Todd and Erin. Charles said they seemed to get along well. "Todd is proud to make good money at the car-leasing company. I'm still concerned because they're both so young. When the classes start, I want Todd to concentrate on his studies," Charles said.

"At least he won't be out all night looking for women and drinking beer," Andrea said.

"He'd better not. It will be nice to see him again when he comes for our wedding. I miss him."

"Of course, you do."

Changing the subject, Charles said, "Today, after we get our marriage license, we're going to the Drake Hotel for lunch. While there, we'll take a look at the rooms that Nana reserved for the ceremony and dinner."

"It's a great day in our lives."

To apply for the marriage license was easy. Both listed that they had been married before and widowed. Charles signed first, then Andrea.

"Now, it's in the records that we intend to marry," he said.

"I can hardly believe it," she said. "So many obstacles have been thrown in our way, but now it's really going to happen."

As they entered the Drake Hotel, Andrea said, "The next time we come here, it will be our wedding day."

"Yes, I can't wait!" He gave her arm a squeeze as they walked up to the reception desk. The manager expected them and said he would show them the reserved rooms. Andrea and Charles followed him.

"Here's the room we've reserved for your ceremony," the manager said. "We'll place chairs on both sides with an aisle in the center. You may decorate the room as you wish."

Both Andrea and Charles approved. Next, the manager showed them the dining room and turned the lights on.

"There's a stage for the musicians, in case you have live music."

"Mrs. Chester has just had surgery, so I'll finalize everything on her behalf," Charles said. "I understand she has decided on the menu, but she wanted me to select the wines."

"I'll let you talk to the bartender. May I show you the bridal suite now?"

Charles turned to Andrea. "Would you like to see it?"

"No, I'm sure it's fine."

Andrea saw the chance to go to the ladies' room while Charles talked to the bartender. She was certain that Charles would pay the bill for the wine and the many extras.

"Is everything to your satisfaction, darling," Charles asked as they sat down to lunch in the dining room.

"Oh yes, this will be so much nicer than the courthouse."

"I've ordered the tickets to Paris. "We'll stay at a hotel on Champs Elysees."

"Wow!"

"It's close to the Arc de Triomphe, the Eiffel Tower, and many other famous sites. Since you haven't been to Paris before, I recommend the Louvre. It's very large, but you should at least see the Mona Lisa."

"Oh, Charles, I'll love it."

"We can enjoy the famous sidewalk cafés and stroll along the Seine."

"It will be fantastic. How will we get to Bordeaux?"

"It's more than 300 miles from Paris, so we'll fly, but once we're there, we can rent a car and drive around the countryside."

"It all sounds so wonderful, Charles."

"You've a valid passport, I hope?"

"I just got a brand new one, but it has my current name."

"It's all right. It matches your driver's license."

They finished their meal. Charles looked at his watch and asked, "Are you ready to go and see your mother?"

"Yes, let's go before the rush hour traffic starts."

Charles found a parking space, and they made their way to the room where Nana recovered from surgery. She was awake with her head resting on the raised back of the bed.

"You look so much better, Nana," Andrea said as she leaned down and kissed her.

"Yes, I know, but my leg hurts almost as much as my chest. I'm admiring all my flowers. Thank you for sending them." Nana talked slowly like it was an effort for her.

"You're welcome. They're from Kathy and Nancy, and the plant is from Charles and me."

"Thank you. It's so nice to see you, Charles. You're not working today?"

"No, I took the day off. We went downtown to get our marriage license. We also looked at the rooms that you've booked for our wedding dinner, Mrs. Chester."

"Good, but please call me Nana. Everyone else does. Jessica started it when she learned to talk. She couldn't say grandma, so she said na-na. I like it."

"I remember," Andrea said.

"How were the rooms?" Nana asked.

"They're perfect," Charles said.

"I'm sorry I won't be able to be there with you."

"Maybe you will," Andrea said.

"When they release me, I'll be going to Kathy's for a while."

"That's good news. I'm so glad you can stay with Kathy."

"The doctor told me that I'd be stronger than before, so I should be able to return to my home."

"Whatever will be best for you, Nana."

Andrea looked at the get-well cards that Nana had received and was surprised to see one from her neighbor, Ernie Anderson.

When the nurse came and said that it was time for medicine and a nap, Andrea and Charles said their good-byes and left.

Chapter 27

While they walked to their car, Charles said he needed to go home and pack a few things for storage. The estate sale was coming up, and everything that was still in his house would be for sale.

"Do you want to come home with me?" he asked?

"Yes, I'd be glad to help you."

"I have the packing material, but I'm not good at packing china and crystal. It's for Todd, you know."

"I remember."

"I need to decide which paintings I want to keep. If you see anything you like, we should set it aside."

Andrea was shocked when she saw how different the house looked. Much of the furniture was gone. Boxes and other packing material were strewn around.

"When are the sales people coming?" she asked.

"They're coming tomorrow to put prices on everything."

"Oh, my goodness, then we'd better get busy." She went up to the china cabinet and opened the glass doors.

"Here's the packing material," Charles said. "Each piece goes in a separate packet. The silverware is already in packets."

"It's easy when we've such great packing material."

When Andrea had finished, Charles came with the silverware, two cartons, and strapping tape. He wrote

"Todd" with a black magic marker on the outside of the cartons.

"I'd like to keep a couple of paintings," he said. "If you don't care for them, I can take them to storage."

"I'll like whatever you like, just bring them to my house."

"Look here," he said, pointing to two oils in big frames. "They're rather large. Do you have room for these on your walls?"

"These are original paintings and much better than what I have, so I'll make room for them."

"You're so accommodating, honey."

"You'll need something to wrap them in. A blanket would be good."

Charles went to the master bedroom and came back with two blankets that he spread on the floor. He lifted the first painting down and placed it on one blanket, and wrapped it up. As he stretched to get the second painting from the wall, it caught on one of the hooks. Charles tumbled to the floor with the large painting on top of him.

"Are you alright, honey?" Andrea stood above him with fear in her eyes.

Charles laughed. "Now, isn't this a comical sight?" he said. "At least I saved the painting."

"You scared the daylight out of me." She lifted the painting off him, so he could get up.

"Are you sure you're all right?"

He touched his hip and limped a few steps. Then he grabbed her and kissed her. "I'm not out of commission yet," he said.

"You could have broken something."

"My bones are still strong, honey, and I can prove it to you."

"I still want to walk around the house to make sure you aren't forgetting anything important. What about photo albums and framed pictures?"

"Matt and Linda took most of them and I've packed the rest."

"What about important documents and papers?"

"I took those to the office."

"Have you gone through all the drawers?"

"No, I haven't. Let's do that."

Charles looked embarrassed. "I didn't think of looking in Elaine's drawers, but I can ask Linda to do it tomorrow. She'll be here all day with the sales people."

"She'd be the right person to do it. She can decide what to do with all her mother's things."

Charles found many odds-and-ends throughout the house that went into various boxes. He stopped to look at some of them, remembering, before he let go.

"You should take your clothes to my house, Charles," Andrea reminded him.

"I can do that tomorrow morning. I'll hang my good suits in a wardrobe and pack the rest in suitcases."

Charles opened the door to the linen closet. It was full of folded linen tablecloths.

"What should I do about the linen?" he asked. "Linda and Cindy said they don't like to iron linen."

"I've a feeling that Erin won't mind. Perhaps it's Irish linen," Andrea said. "Let's save a tablecloth or two for her and Todd. We could take it to my house and give it to them for Christmas."

"Now, there's an idea. I might have all the Christmas gifts I need right here," Charles said with a hopeful smile.

"Well, maybe not all of them," Andrea mumbled as she selected two table clothes for Todd. One would fit the kitchen table that she had given them; the other would have to wait for the dining room table that they would own some day.

"Since we'll have big dinners, we might need an extra large tablecloth," Andrea said.

"Take what you want, darling."

Andrea selected one that would fit her extended dining table. It belonged to Charles, she reasoned.

"Aren't you tired yet, honey?" Charles asked as he stood and looked at her.

"Yes, I'm getting a little tired."

"Let's have a glass of wine."

When he came back with the wine, he said it was a good thing he had remembered his wine cellar.

"Surely there must be room in your basement for several cases of good wine?" he said.

"Of course, honey. We can put it in the cold storage part. Let's take one bottle of wine home with us."

"Then I can bring the cases over tomorrow."

"Don't you feel bad about dismantling your home, Charles?"

"Not particularly. Downsizing is necessary sometimes. It actually feels good to leave some of my past behind and go forward with you, darling."

"What impresses me the most is that not once have you called me Elaine."

"And you haven't called me Philip either."

"But we call each other honey and darling a lot."

"Yes, that's safe, I guess, but seriously, you don't remind me of Elaine. You're just you, sweet, sweet Andrea."

"And you're Charles, the new man in my life. I couldn't be happier."

"I'm sorry about all the practicalities, but I've had enough of packing for today."

"You're doing it for me, so I can't complain."

"You're worth the trouble, but it's been a long day. Can we go home now?" *He said home!*

"Yes, but first I want to see what you have in your fridge and freezer that we can have for dinner. I haven't had time to go shopping."

"You do that, honey, and I'll take these paintings to the car."

Andrea packed food in a carton and added the wine bottle. Charles placed the paintings between the seats in his car and came back for the food. He turned the burglar alarm on before they left.

As he drove, Charles concentrated on the traffic that had grown to rush-hour strength and took side roads to avoid the worst snarls.

Andrea unlocked her door and carried in the food while Charles brought in the paintings.

"Where should I put them?" he asked.

"In the den. I'll fix some food for us."

Charles was moving in with her. Everything was wonderful except Nana's illness. After they had eaten, Andrea snuggled up to Charles on the living room couch.

"I hope I haven't bossed you around too much today, honey," she said.

"Not at all, I appreciated your help. Without you, it would have been so much harder."

"I wish you didn't have to spend one more night at that house alone. It's not good for you."

"I'd be glad to stay here tonight."

"Then you'll have to go back in the morning."

"I can do that."

"What time are the salespeople coming?"

"Linda knows and she'll let them in. The sale is Friday and Saturday."

"What happens with anything that is left after the sale?"

"It will be sold elsewhere. The house will be empty when they leave. Then I'll send in a cleaning crew."

"It's amazing what you have to go through to marry me. I feel guilty."

"You shouldn't. I love marrying you."

"I'm the luckiest of us two." They kissed until passion overtook them both. Then he lifted her up and carried her to the bedroom.

"You're not supposed to carry me over the threshold until after we're married," Andrea said.

"Why not, we've done everything else before marriage.

Chapter 28

In the morning when Charles had left the house, Andrea still felt the warmth and love from the night before as she went to the living room to remove her wedding picture.

I'm sorry, Phil, but you have to move to Jessica's place. She glanced at the picture one last time. How young and innocent they looked. They had been younger than Jessica was now. She placed the framed picture on top of other pictures and albums in a box that she would take to her daughter. In the den, she looked at Charles' oil paintings that were propped up against the wall. She tried to make out the signature of the artist. The paintings must be valuable. Everything that Charles owned was valuable.

She was ready to head for work when Jessica called. Andrea could hear her daughter sniffling.

"Do you have a cold, honey?" she asked.

"No, I'm crying."

"Why are you crying?"

"Jason and I had a fight. He stormed out this morning."

"I'm sorry to hear that. Do you want to tell me about it over lunch?"

"Yeah, thanks, Mom."

"We can get some fast food and sit in the car and talk."

"Alright, I'll stop outside the bookstore at one o'clock, but I'm not coming in."

"That's fine, Jessica. Try to calm down. I'm sure that everything will be alright again between you two."

Andrea wondered what they could be fighting about and hoped it wasn't anything serious?

Why did everything have to happen at once? Nana's heart attack, and now this....

Andrea looked out the window to see if Jessica's car was there. It was five after and still no sign of her. Perhaps Jason had come home and they had made up. At ten after, Jessica drove into the parking lot.

Andrea told Bob she would be having lunch with her daughter.

"Climb in, Mom." Jessica said through her open car window.

Andrea buckled up and waited for Jessica to talk. She didn't seem upset at the moment. Jessica asked how Nana was doing.

"She's doing well, but you should go and see her."

"I will. I suppose she won't be able to come to your wedding?"

"We don't think she'll be well enough."

"That's too bad. I don't think that Jason will come either." Andrea looked at her daughter and asked, "Are you arguing about something serious?"

They were at the fast-food place and Jessica chose the drive-up window to order. Once they had their food, she parked the car, and began to talk.

"We argued about the computer work I'm doing for him. He said I wasn't doing it right. I don't know as much

225

about data programs as he does, but I'm trying hard to learn. Then one thing led to another. He even blamed me for spending too much money on clothes, but, but," she stammered, "I can't use the same clothes all the time when I'm teaching."

Jessica snapped her pop can open and drank through a straw. It hurt Andrea to see her daughter's beautiful blue eyes filling up with tears.

"Arguments have a tendency to escalate on both sides. Did you blame him for anything?"

"I said he wasn't contributing enough for groceries, that he left his dirty socks on the floor, and didn't help with the laundry."

Andrea took a sip of her coffee that had cooled down enough so she could drink it.

"All that is trivial, Jessica," she said. "It has nothing to do with how you feel for each other. Do you still love him?"

"I love him. That's why I'm upset, isn't it?" Jessica looked at her mother.

"Yes, that's why you're upset and that's why Jason stormed out. He still loves you."

"Oh, Mom, you sure can put things in perspective. You always calm me down when I'm sad, just like when I was a little girl."

"That's one of the things that mothers are for."

They ate their hamburgers and finished their drinks.

"I don't suppose that you and Charles have quarreled yet?" Jessica said.

"Actually, we have, but we made up right away. It was a misunderstanding."

"Charles is a wonderful man."

"Jason is too, but he's young and perhaps not as patient with women yet. He might still want to be the quarterback he was in college, call the plays, or whatever name they have for it."

Jessica laughed. "It's part of his appeal. He's is resolute, a decision maker, and it makes him successful at what he does."

"Although I'm surprised he leaves his socks on the floor. Don't pick them up. He'll get the hint when there're no clean socks in his drawer," Andrea said.

Jessica laughed again.

"It's good to see you laugh, daughter."

"Well, maybe I'm getting over my PMS. It can get me in trouble. I should apologize to him."

"When you do, I'm sure he'll do the same."

"Thanks, Mom. I'll take you back to the bookstore."

As Jessica dropped her off, she asked, "Mom, can I move back home for a while if Jason is unreasonable?"

Andrea hesitated for a second, but then assured Jessica, "Of course, you can, at least until Charles and I marry."

"Then I'll get my own place if it comes down to that."

Andrea couldn't stop thinking about Jessica. Jason had rented the apartment in his name. If they separated, Jessica would be the one moving out. It would not be a good time for her to move back home. She felt guilt over her own happiness while Jessica was unhappy, but she calmed her fears by saying to herself that school would start in September. Jessica would be back to teaching. Things will get back to normal.

On her afternoon break, Andrea went to the backroom to call Charles.

"Honey, I hate to tell you this, but Jessica and Jason are quarreling, and I'm afraid that Jessica might want to move back home."

Charles took a few seconds to take it all in. "I'm sorry to hear that. Do you think it's serious?"

"It's the usual arguments, money, work, and socks on the floor."

"They'll probably make up, at least I hope so, but until it blows over I can stay at my house. I can shut my door and tell the sales people not to touch anything. My bed, my clothes and shoes are still there."

"And I was so looking forward to you moving in with me."

"I was too, but let's give Jessica and Jason a little time and we'll see what happens. I can still bring over my wine boxes and tools tonight, can't I?"

"Of course, I'm expecting you."

When Jessica called the next day, Andrea asked, "Did you talk to Jason yet?"

"At first, he didn't answer his cell phone, and he didn't come home last night. I left a voice mail asking him to come home so we could talk. When he finally came, he said he needed time alone, so he packed his things and left. I apologized, but he said it wasn't my fault. He would go and stay with a friend for a while. Oh mom, I'm heart-broken."

"I'm sorry, honey, but don't give up. He'll probably miss you after a while and come back."

"I hope so."

Jessica's problem was something that Andrea didn't want to deal with at the moment. At least Jason was the one moving out, and Jessica would still be in the apartment.

Andrea gave Charles a call during her lunch hour and asked, "How did it go this morning?"

"I had to stay and help Linda for the better part of the day. Then I went to the storage place with Todd's things. Linda will take care of the rest. The wine cases and tools are in my car."

"Good. Bring it all. I've bad news and good news to report. The bad new is that Jason has moved out. The good news is that Jessica can stay in their apartment."

"I still hope they'll work it out before our wedding, and I hope Jessica will be one of our witnesses."

"I hope so too. By the way, Kristian and his bride are arriving soon in Chicago, so we need to invite them to our wedding."

"Of course. Speaking of our wedding, the last two nights before our big day, I'll be at the same hotel as my brother and his family in Arlington Heights. There'll be six adults coming from Denver, so I'll send a limo for them. I'll pick up Todd and Erin myself. They're staying with Linda and Ed."

"So Erin is coming?"

"Yes, she's coming. This time she won't be a stranger."

"When do they arrive?"

"Next Thursday."

"I've taken tomorrow off from work, so I can go and see Nana, but I'm sorry I have to work over the week-end," Andrea said.

"It's all right. I need to make up for lost time at the office. Papers have piled up on my desk."

Charles put a positive spin on Jessica's and Jason's separation. "It might even be good for them to be apart for a while," he said.

Bob came into the back room, and Andrea quickly said goodbye to Charles and put away her phone.

"It's getting close to your wedding," Bob said.

"Yes." She hastened to add, "It's only going to be family, about 25 people. I doubt that my mother will be strong enough to come."

"That's too bad. She would have enjoyed it."

Chapter 29

Charles came dressed in jeans.

"Welcome to our home, honey," Andrea said, as she threw her arms around him.

"Thanks, darling, but I'm afraid I'm sweaty. It's hot outside."

"Sweaty or not, you're my husband-to-be." Having taken the wine cases down to the basement, he picked some tools from his toolbox to hang his paintings. He searched for studs and drilled holes for hooks. Each painting needed two large hooks to keep them straight.

"Are they French paintings?" Andrea asked.

"Yes, I bought them at an auction. The artist is not that famous yet, but I think he will be."

"I like the landscape the best," Andrea said. The other one was a still-life painting.

With the work accomplished, they sat down to admire the art.

"We can buy more art when we go over there," Charles said. "The artists sitting by the Seine will do your portrait if you like."

"I can't wait to go there."

Charles' cell phone rang. It was Linda. Andrea understood that Charles tried to solve a problem over the phone, but gave up.

"Sorry, honey, but I must go back to the house and help Linda."

Andrea followed him to the hall, pulled out a drawer, and retrieved a house key."

"Here, you should have your own key, honey."

"Thanks, I'll move the toolbox to the garage when I get back."

"Dinner will be ready."

They kissed hastily, and he was off.

Andrea had a grilled chicken waiting in the refrigerator. She put new, small potatoes in a pot and covered them with water.

While she waited, for Charles she called Jessica, who complained about how empty the apartment seemed without Jason. "It's so weird," she said. "Jason has left me and Charles is moving in with you." Andrea told her daughter not to give up on Jason.

"I don't think he'll change his mind before your wedding, so don't count on him to attend," Jessica said.

"That's too bad. We can't count on Nana either, but Kristian and Marie are coming."

"How long will you continue to work, Mom?"

I might resign from my job. Do you think I could get a part-time position as a teacher's aide?" Andrea asked.

"Well, you do have a degree in English, so if there's an opening, I can't see why you couldn't be a candidate."

"Charles says I can do anything I want, but he's not in favor of my working on weekends."

"I can understand that, Mom. I'll inquire for you. It might not be at my school."

"It doesn't have to be your school. I could volunteer. I'll need something to occupy my time."

Still no call from Charles. He hadn't moved in yet, and here she was already missing him so much. She turned on the TV and listened to the news. It was the usual bad news from Iraq and Afghanistan with more American soldiers killed. So far, there had been no draft. Every soldier was a volunteer, but more and more young men and women who had signed up for the National Guard or National Reserve to help pay for college now risked being sent overseas to fight.

Andrea saw Charles' toolbox where he had put it and grabbed it by the handle to move it out of the way.

"Ouch! My back." She felt a sharp pain in her lower back. Worse yet, she couldn't straighten out, and this just days before her wedding. Multiple scenarios rushed through her mind. Nana was expecting her tomorrow.

What can I do? If only Charles would come. He had his own key. I'm so glad I gave it to him. Where's my phone? In my purse, and it's sitting there on the shelf, where I can't reach it. If I only had something to pull it down with?

Lying on the floor with her head near the door to the hall closet, she thought of the cane that Philip had used toward the end of his life. It was in the left corner of the closet. If she could get to it, she could use the handle to pull down her purse on the floor. The closet door was slightly ajar. Inch by inch, she slid it open. Relief flooded through her when she felt the cane standing up against the wall, just where she had put it two years ago. Now she had the tool she needed. In a few seconds, the purse was next to her on the floor.

She retrieved her phone and speed-dialed Charles who answered right away.

"I'm sorry, I'll be late for dinner," he said.

"Charles, dinner is not the problem. The problem is that my back has gone out, and I can't get up from the floor."

"Oh no. What happened?"

"I tried to lift your toolbox."

"You didn't. It's my fault. I'll be right there."

While she waited, she used the cane to pull herself up on a nearby stool. It felt good to be off the floor. She leaned on the cane and looked at her watch every five minutes until she heard his car in her driveway and his key turning the lock in the door.

"Honey, how bad is it?" he asked as he rushed toward her.

"Please carry me to my bed," she said.

"Don't you think I should take you to the hospital?"

"No, just get me the icepack from the freezer, please."

He put her down on the bed as gently as he could. It hurt, but she thought she would be all right.

Charles came with the blue icepack and a towel around it and slid it underneath her back.

"I got the icepack after my accident," she said.

"I know, because I got one when I went to see my doctor. Oh, honey, I'm so sorry I didn't move the toolbox to the garage before I left."

"I didn't know it was so heavy," she said.

"Good that you had the phone with you," he said.

"Well, it was in my purse, and I found a way to get to it. I feel better already. Tell me about the problem at your house."

"Well, first we had some disputes with the salespeople. They didn't know how to price some of the valuables. Then on top of that, Susan showed up. That's why Linda called."

"What did Susan want?"

"She wanted the crystal chandelier in the dining room. I told her she would have to come and buy it at the estate sale, but she wanted it for nothing. Well, I'm fair, but 'nothing' won't be fair to my children. When we finally agreed on a price, I told her that she would have to take it down herself before morning, or it would be sold. Of course, she didn't know how to do that. Linda suggested we put a 'Sold' sign on it, and that's what we did. Now, she'll have to pay the sales people to get it."

"Serves her right. I suppose Susan ranted about me, too."

"Yes, she did. Sorry about that honey."

"If you help me, I'll try to sit up."

Sitting on the edge of the bed, she tried to stand, but sat down again.

"Please get me the cane from the hallway," she said.

When Charles returned with the cane, he asked, "Where did you get this?"

"It was Philip's. It got me up from the floor."

"You're so resourceful, darling. Do you think you can walk now?"

"Yes, let's go to the kitchen," she said. "There's a grilled chicken in the fridge. You must be hungry, and I am too."

With the cane in one hand and Charles supporting her, she limped to the kitchen and sat down.

"I'll be alright," she said. "It's the first time my back has gone out, but it has happened to Nana a couple of times. She got over it, and so will I."

"I think I'd better stay the night to make sure you're alright. I'll move the toolbox to the garage after dinner. What do we do about the potatoes?"

"If you don't want to wait for them, you can put the pot in the fridge for tomorrow."

"I think the chicken is enough for tonight," Charles said.

Chapter 30

In the morning, Andrea felt better but applied the ice-pack before getting up.

Charles started the coffee and went to the stoop to get the newspaper. Andrea's flowers greeted him in vibrant colors, and the birds chirped. It would be a beautiful day. He drew in a long breath of fragrant air when he saw the neighbor stepping out to retrieve his paper. The man looked a little surprised to see Charles, but said, "Good morning."

"Good morning," Charles said and walked toward the man with his hand outstretched. "I guess I should introduce myself. I'm Charles Bordeaux, Andrea's fiancé."

"Well, nice to meet you, Mr. Bordeaux. "I'm Ernie Anderson. I guess congratulations are in order then."

"Thank you. We'll be neighbors, so you can call me Charles."

"Welcome to the neighborhood, Charles." The elderly man shook Charles' hand.

"Please call me Ernie. When is the wedding?"

"This Saturday. It will be a civil ceremony and a small gathering of the family."

"Good luck then and my best wishes to Andrea."

"I'll convey your greeting to her. Good to meet you, Ernie."

Charles went to the bedroom to see how Andrea was doing. She was done with the icepack.

"I feel much better," she said.

"I think you should call your doctor, honey, and we'll take it from there."

"First I want to get up and see how it feels."

Andrea got up by herself and limped just a little bit. She left the bathroom door open in case she needed help. When she came to the kitchen, she wore her robe.

"Oh, you're walking. That's great. There's hope for our wedding yet."

"Don't worry about it. I'll be fine."

"That's good to hear, honey. I just met your neighbor."

Charles was reading the paper and looked at Andrea above his glasses.

"Ernie?"

"Yes, Ernie. He sent his best wishes to you. I told him we'll marry on Saturday and that we would be neighbors."

"He's a nice retired man of Swedish extraction. You can almost see it by looking at him. By the way, I think he's a little sweet on Nana."

"That's an interesting tidbit."

"Nothing serious, I'm sure. Anyhow, I should ask him to keep watch over my house while we're gone on our honeymoon."

After breakfast, Andrea called her doctor's office and asked to speak to the nurse. The nurse spoke to the doctor and called back. She said that back ailments were common. Andrea should continue to apply ice. There was no need for bed rest, but she should avoid lifting. When Andrea asked if she could go to work, the advice was that it would be best to stay home for the next few days. If she was not better by Monday, she should come in and be checked. For now, she could get a prescription for pain medication, but Andrea declined. She would make do with over-the-counter pills.

Jessica called and said she had seen the announcement in the paper about their marriage license.

"Really? I haven't read the paper yet."

"I always check to see who's getting married and now it's my mother," Jessica said, emphasizing the word mother.

Andrea turned to Charles and said, "There's something in the paper about us getting married."

Charles looked surprised, but began to turn the pages.

"Here it is. It just says that we've applied for a marriage license." Andrea came and read it over his shoulder.

Jessica was still on the phone.

"Mom, I've something else to tell you. You can go and apply for a part-time job as a teacher's aide at my school. It's for Kindergarten."

"Thank you, Jessica. I don't know when I'll be able to do it because my back went out last night." She told Jessica how it had happened.

"Oh no!"

"It's not that bad. I'm better already, but I don't think I should go and see Nana today as planned. She'll understand because she has had the same problem with her back."

"I could go instead of you. I've planned to go one of these days," Jessica said.

"Oh, that's perfect. I'll call her and tell her. She'll be happy to see you."

"Take it easy, Mom. You have to get well for your wedding, you know."

Andrea told Jessica not to worry. The wedding was not for another week. Jason was still absent. Jessica no longer worked for him.

Andrea dreaded to call Bob and tell him she needed two sick days. As expected, it put him in a difficult situation. If Trudy couldn't work, he would have to fill in, and it was his turn to have his sons over the weekend. Andrea said she was sorry. She could get a statement from her doctor on Monday if he needed one, but she hoped to be able to work on Monday afternoon.

"Get well soon. We need you here at the store," Bob said.

Andrea hung up the phone and breathed a sigh of relief. "It went better than I thought," she said.

"Do you think you'll be alright alone this morning? I can come back for lunch if you need me," Charles said.

"I'll be fine, but I was so glad you could come and rescue me last night."

"I'm grateful you're better. If you need me today, give me a call. I want you to carry your cell phone in your pocket all the time."

"Luckily, I have pockets today."

"Now, let's put your cell phone in one of those pockets. And if you change clothes, don't forget to move your phone."

"Do you have your key, honey?"

"Yes, I do. I'll be back tonight."

Charles spent the weekend with Andrea while she recovered. On Monday morning, she felt well enough to go to Jessica's school and apply for the position as a teacher's aide. In the afternoon, she went back to work. It was the week of their wedding.

On Wednesday, Charles packed his suitcases and garment bags with everything he needed for the wedding and honeymoon. Then he left his house for the last time and checked in at the hotel in Arlington Heights.

On Thursday, he called Andrea and invited her to a French restaurant in Arlington Heights on Friday evening. It would be a rehearsal dinner, he said. Jessica was also invited. "It will give you a chance to meet my brother and his family before the wedding. I'm sorry to spring this on you so late, darling," Charles said.

"It's all right. I like to meet your brother and his family. I'm just wondering what I should wear?"

"Anything you have. You don't need anything new for this. How about the blue dress? It looks good on you, and it will remind me of our first date."

"The blue dress it is. Did Todd and Erin arrive?"

"Yes, they did. I'll pick you up, darling."

"What time?"

"At six o'clock. Then we'll go and get Jessica. Jason is not in the picture, is he?"

"No, I think our wedding put too much pressure on him, and that's why he's staying away."

"Then he might come back later."

"I hope so. I'll be waiting for you, honey."

Charles escorted Andrea and Jessica to their reserved tables and introduced them to his brother Paul and his wife Leslie, their grown sons Shawn and Justin, and their wives. There were many people with the last name of Bordeaux. Everyone except Charles and Nancy was new to Jessica. Kathy and Roger had sent their regrets because of a conflict. Charles' mother was there, and so were Matt and Cindy with their children, and Linda and Ed with their boys. Andrea enjoyed seeing Erin and Todd again. Erin looked great in a peasant-style skirt and scarlet red blouse. Todd proudly introduced her to everyone who hadn't met her. Charles had placed Jessica beside Todd and Erin, and they appeared to have a good time together.

Paul proposed a toast to Charles and Andrea. They dined on Norwegian Salmon that everyone praised. The large selection of side dishes and desserts made it difficult to choose. Andrea nibbled on the food and sipped the wine. Charles beamed and gave a short speech.

"You won't believe how many hoops I had to jump through to sell my house and move out, but it was all worth it. At least I didn't have to buy a new house right away, because I'm moving in with Andrea. I'm so lucky to have found her. From our own experience, we know that it's possible to fall in love after 50. Now, I just want my relatives to welcome Andrea into our family." He ended by thanking Paul and Leslie for the wonderful dinner.

Chapter 31

Andrea's suitcase was packed and ready for her honeymoon. Morning showers had cooled the air and watered the dry ground. They needed rain, but why on her wedding day? She scanned the overcast sky from her front stoop. The weather report predicted clearing in the afternoon, and she hoped it was correct.

As Andrea was about to go back in the house, Jessica arrived in a cab. She carried a dress bag and a shoebox.

"I didn't expect you to arrive in a cab," Andrea said.

"I had to because I'm not coming back here tonight."

"I didn't think of that."

"Today is your big day, Mom," she said.

"I only wish that Nana could be present."

"I can say the same for Jason," Jessica said with a sigh.

"I know. Do you want a cup of tea?"

"Yes, please."

Andrea had a pot ready and they sat down to talk.

"Did you enjoy last night?" Andrea asked.

"I enjoyed it a lot," Jessica said. "It was a fabulous dinner."

"How did you like Todd?"

"He's great. I had a good time with Todd and Erin. I think you'll have fantastic new relatives, Mom."

"Yes, I think so, too, and Charles is the cream of the crop."

"Are you nervous, Mom? You're looking at the clock all the time."

"I'm not nervous, but I think we should start dressing."

"Okay, I'll rinse out the tea pot."

"Would you please help me zip up my dress?" Andrea asked.

"Yes, of course, Mom. I like that lime-green color on you," Jessica said as she admired the dress.

The neckline on the satiny bodice dipped modestly in the front. Silvery lace covered the ballerina length skirt. The long, flaring sleeves were made of the same lace.

"It's gorgeous, Mom," Jessica said.

Andrea's auburn hair had grown long enough to reach below her ears. She had decided against a hat. Instead, she fastened a clasp decorated with silk flowers by one ear. Turning her head in front of the mirror, she asked Jessica, "Does this look right to you, honey?"

"It looks fine, but let me help you fasten it better, Mom."

While Jessica brushed her long, blond hair, Andrea slipped into white heels with closed toes. Last, she put on the pearl necklace and matching pearl earrings that had been a gift from her mother. Her dress was complete. Swirling her skirt in front of the long mirror, she flipped the wide sleeves that reached half way down her hands. The diamonds in her ring sparkled.

"I hope the dress is appropriate for my age," she said.

"It is. Charles will be impressed," Jessica assured her.

Jessica looked marvelous in her emerald-green dress with spaghetti-straps that exposed her shoulders, her back, and her long, bare legs. Her red toenails showed in open black sandals. Her hair cascaded around her face. Andrea suspected her daughter had chosen the style of dress so that no one would mistake her for the bride.

The sun had come out and the temperature gauge showed a perfect 82 degrees. When the limo drove up the driveway, Andrea clutched her pearl-covered evening bag and was ready for her big day.

Jessica told the limo driver to pick up the suitcase that stood inside the door. "It will go to the bridal suite," she said.

The limo moved fast in the outside lane. As they approached the city, the haze obscured the Chicago skyline ahead. After a while, the familiar shape of the Hancock Tower became visible. Andrea's thoughts went to Nana at Mt. Sinai not far from the city's center. She still worried about her.

The limo stopped outside Drake, and the driver opened the doors for them. A porter took Andrea's suitcase and led the way. When the bride and bridesmaid entered the wedding room, the guests stood up and applauded. Cindy waited inside the door with her children.

"You're adorable," Andrea said to Ellen and Danny.

Cindy handed Andrea a bridal bouquet of tulips that reminded her of the first flowers she had received from Charles, only these were hot pink.

"You look fantastic," Cindy said with an admiring look at Andrea.

"Thank you. So do you, Cindy." Cindy wore a midnight blue dress with a slit skirt.

"Ellen will be your flower girl and Danny the ring bearer," Cindy said. "I'll be your Matron of Honor and Jessica your bridesmaid."

"What a surprise to have so many attending me," Andrea said. She looked up and saw Charles and Matt standing at the opposite end of the room. Both were dressed in white tuxedos. The judge, who just joined them, wore a black robe. Flowers decorated the room. A photographer stood by the wall. It's almost like a church wedding. Andrea thought. She felt the excitement rising within her.

The music started. Andrea had not expected music, but now she heard the first stanzas of "*Here Comes the Bride.*"

Cindy lined up the children, Danny first, then Ellen. Ellen carried a flower basket. Cindy came next, then the bride. Andrea didn't need anyone to give her away. She looked straight ahead with Jessica behind her. Matt filmed from the front and a photographer from the back of the room. The distance was short. Andrea looked at Charles, who had a big smile on his face. He came to her side and they joined hands. "You're a beautiful bride," he whispered.

They promised to love each other for the rest of their lives, which was what they had agreed on for their vows. They exchanged their wedding bands. Andrea's had a row of diamonds. Judge Dickenson proclaimed them husband and wife.

"Charles, my friend, you may kiss the bride." he said. Charles lifted Andrea off the floor and planted a big kiss on her mouth.

"Congratulations. May I present Mr. and Mrs. Charles Bordeaux," the judge said. Andrea smiled broadly and so did Charles.

"I'm so happy to have you as my wife, darling," Charles whispered as he put his arm around her and looked adoringly at her. "I'm glad to be your wife," she whispered back.

Andrea's eyes fell on the guests and among them was Nana in a wheelchair. "Nana is here!" she said to Charles. "That makes me even happier." Andrea blew a kiss to Nana while they walked back the aisle to greet the guests.

Kristian and Marie caught her eye. It was the first time Andrea had seen the suntanned, blond and beautiful Marie.

Roger and Kathy came with Nana in a wheelchair as the first in the reception line. Nana's cheeks were rouged and she wore a corsage.

"I'm so glad you could come, Nana," Andrea said as she bent down and kissed her.

"I'm glad to be here, and I'm so happy for you," Nana said.

Andrea turned to Kathy. "Thank you for taking Nana in."

"That's what I wanted to do. It's about time I do something for her. We picked her up yesterday. That's why we couldn't come to the rehearsal dinner."

Charles talked to Nana and bent down to kiss her on the cheek.

"Congratulations to the both of you," Nana said. "I told the doctors I didn't want to miss my daughter's wedding, so they released me. I love your dress, Andrea."

"It means the world to me that you're here, Nana."

"Thank you for bringing her," Andrea said to Roger. "It makes everything perfect." Charles' mother was next in line. She said she was glad to have Andrea as her new daughter-in-law. It meant a lot to Andrea.

When Matt and Cindy came up to them, Andrea told Cindy that she had been greatly surprised at having both a flower girl and a ring-bearer at the ceremony.

"It was meant to be a surprise," Cindy said.

Jessica stood beside the bridal couple and greeted everyone with hugs and kisses. When the turn came to the newlywed Kristian and Marie, she welcomed them heartily to Chicago. The newlywed couples congratulated each other on their marriages.

"I'm so glad to meet you, Marie. I've heard so much from Jessica about your wonderful wedding," Andrea said.

"I'm glad to be able to attend yours," Marie said in accented but beautiful English." Kristian had a big grin on his face as he hugged Andrea and kissed her. She didn't think he looked quite as much like Phil as before. Perhaps it had been her imagination.

"Will you entertain Jessica while Charles and I are on our honeymoon?" she whispered to Kristian.

"Yes, we'll be glad to."

"Hope you'll like living here in Chicago," Charles said. He and Marie were the same height. Both Charles and Andrea expressed their delight in having her and Kristian attending their wedding.

Cindy posed for the photographer with her children. "Did you hire a photographer, Charles?" Andrea asked.

"Guilty as charged."

Nancy stood in front of them. "Congrats. I'm so happy for you, sis," she said, hugging her. "I'll help Kathy with Nana." Nancy's girls wore pretty dresses. Linda and Ed came with their pre-teen boys. Andrea didn't want to embarrass the boys by kissing them, so she put a hand on their shoulders as she said, "Glad to have you here." She was also happy to see Paul and Leslie again.

"Congratulations. You and Charles must come out to Denver and visit us," Paul said.

"We'd love to come," Andrea assured him. Shawn, Justin, and their wives came next. Last in line were Todd and Erin. Erin wore a youthful, sky-blue dress that flattered her slender figure. She hugged Andrea, and Charles kissed Erin on the cheek and said she looked great in blue.

When they had greeted all the guests, Andrea and Jessica excused themselves and went to the ladies' room. Charles waited for them in the foyer as they came out.

"Are we waiting for someone else?" Andrea asked.

"I don't think so. I just want to look at my beautiful wife. That dress is very becoming on you. Judge Dickenson said that you're knockout beautiful."

"Charles, I don't believe that, but thank you, honey, for arranging the wonderful ceremony. It was much more than I had expected."

"I'm glad you're pleased. Shall we go in now, Mrs. Bordeaux?"

Andrea smiled at hearing her new name. "Yes, I'm ready." She walked in on Charles' arm carrying her bouquet.

Chapter 32

Everyone applauded as the bride and groom entered the dining room. The video cameras rolled. Andrea felt moved by it all. She blinked away tears as she and Charles sat down at the head table flanked by their mothers. There were hot-pink tulips on all the tables.

Tulips in August!

Andrea had a hard time concentrating on the food, but Charles said it was very good and that she should eat more so she would last a long time. "There will be no food in the honeymoon suite until morning," he said.

Paul proposed the first toast. Then it was Matt's turn. Both welcomed Andrea to the family, Roger spoke on behalf of his mother-in-law and proposed a toast to Nana's speedy recovery before toasting the bridal couple and welcoming Charles as his brother-in-law. Ed described how Charles and Andrea had met, as if they didn't know. Andrea had to admit he was funny.

While Andrea and Charles cut the wedding cake, two musicians appeared on stage, a piano player and a violin player.

"Are we expected to dance?" Andrea asked Charles. "We've never danced together. Do you even know how to dance?"

"I haven't done it lately, but I don't think it's something you forget. It's like riding a bike. I think I can waltz around the floor with you a few times before my legs stiffen up. And that's no joke," he said.

"I haven't danced for a long time either. We're both out of practice."

"I can't wait to take you to the bridal suite," he said.

"Hush, Charles. I'll stuff this cake in your mouth so you can't talk so much."

"It's your turn now to be quiet," he said as he fed her a piece of cake. They rinsed it down with champagne and kissed while the photographer snapped pictures.

The violin player announced, "The wedding waltz. Would Mr. and Mrs. Bordeaux please come to the floor?"

Charles took Andrea's arm and walked up to the dance floor with a self-assured swagger. When the music started, Andrea found it easy to follow his moves. Why hadn't they done this before? After a few turns, she asked, "Are you stiff yet?"

"No, not yet, but I want to save my energy for tonight."

He motioned to the musicians to stop. "Now, we invite everyone who wants to dance to do so and enjoy the evening. My wife and I are going to retire early because we're flying to Paris tomorrow morning."

The men booed him. "We don't buy the part about retiring early," Ed shouted. The photographer said that they couldn't leave yet. First, he had to take the official pictures.

"Just a minute," Charles said. "I do want to thank everyone for coming, and a special thank you to my mother-in-law, Margaret Chester, or Nana, as we affectionately call her, for hosting this dinner. We love you and wish you a speedy recovery. We love you all."

The photographer snapped pictures of the bridal couple alone, the wedding party, and together with all the guests. It took a long while before they were finished.

Then Charles asked for all the unmarried women to line up for the throwing of the bouquet. Nancy, Jessica, and Erin answered the call. Andrea threw the bouquet so that Jessica caught it with ease. Everyone applauded, and Andrea hoped that Jessica would get married to Jason after all.

When the music began to play rock-and-roll, all the kids and teenagers descended on the dance floor. Charles and Andrea saw the opportunity to say goodbye to their mothers and the other adults before retreating to their bridal suite.

As they rode the elevator to their floor, Charles told Andrea that he had added international calling to his cell phone and that they could text Kathy to find out how Nana was doing while they were away and Kathy could text them.

"It's a great comfort to me to be able to be in touch with them," Andrea said. I appreciate that very much."

Charles put the key card in the lock and they entered the room that had a view of the lit-up shoreline. "We don't have to close the drapes," he said. There's only Lake Michigan outside."

"Are you sure there aren't any photographers in here?"

"I'm sure."

"I've never been photographed so much in my life."

"Neither have I. It feels good to be alone."

"I agree, but I really enjoyed our wedding day."

"It isn't over yet, darling. Look here," Charles said, pointing to the king-sized bed. "Quite a difference from your double bed."

Charles had already taken off his coat and tie when she went to the bathroom with her red lingerie in one hand. When she made her entry, Charles had dimmed the lights and turned on romantic music. He lay propped up on pillows in the bed, waiting for her.

Unsnapping her red bra, she whisked it away with a flip of her wrist. Turning around, she lowered her tiny red panties one inch at the time while wiggling her hips to the beat of the music.

"I didn't know I had married a stripper," Charles said with a grin, "but I'm enjoying the show." He cupped his head in his hands.

"Well, you didn't have a bachelor party, did you, honey?" she said as she faced him and kicked off the last thread.

"No, I did not. This is much better. Come here, darling. You're driving me crazy." He grabbed hold of her and pulled her down on top of him, holding her tight. "Stay here. This is where I want you, darling."

She rubbed his bare chest. His voice thickened as he told her how much he loved her.

"I love you just as much," she said.

"I like to take it slow and make it last," he said.

"That's not what you're doing," she said.

As usual, their passion overpowered them.

"Oh, Charles," she whispered. "What a wedding night!"

"We're not done yet," he said.

She licked her swollen lips.

"It was our best time yet," she said.

"We saved it for our wedding night. This is wonderful. I hate to think how lonely I'd be without you."

"I didn't know what I was missing."

"Love the second time around is good."

"Amazingly so. I had no idea I could fall in love after 50."

"Neither did I. Neither did I."

They slept until it was light outside and Lake Michigan appeared in all its grandeur outside their window. Charles reached for the drawer in his night table and retrieved a small gift-wrapped box.

"My morning gift to you, Mrs. Bordeaux."

"Honey, you're spoiling me," she said.

"I love to spoil you."

The box contained earrings that matched her engagement ring. "Oh, Charles, they're beautiful. Thank you so much. My wedding band is also very special."

"But then you're very special to me."

"And you're just as precious to me. I'll wear the earrings to Paris, but I'm a bit afraid of losing them."

"They're insured and so are your rings."

She looked at her rings and at his ring. "I like that they are different from the ones we had before."

"These rings are ours." They intertwined their fingers, and Charles kissed the inside of her hand.

"For the rest of our lives."

"For the rest of our lives."

Charles looked at his watch, and said, "I've ordered room service for breakfast."

"Oh, Charles, what time is the food coming? I don't want the waiter to surprise us in bed."

"In about one minute."

Andrea jumped up and went to the bathroom, carrying her box with the new earrings and sweeping up her lingerie from the floor.

"Get up, honey, before the food comes," she said to Charles as she turned around. "You need to open the door."

"Not until I've moved the 'Do not disturb' sign."

Andrea busied herself in the bathroom until breakfast had arrived. She put her earrings on in front of the mirror and moved her head so that they dangled and glistened. Then she walked out wearing a mini-length morning wrap. The corners of her mouth turned up as she smiled. He saw the earrings right away, smiled, and kissed her.

"They look good on you, darling," he said. "Are you ready to eat?"

"Yes, I'm hungry."

"We used up a lot of calories last night."

She lifted the lids and smelled the food. "Eggs Benedict," she said.

"Bon appetite."

"Do you speak French?"

"A little. My father spoke the language, so I took it in high school and college. But I've forgotten most of it."

"I took Latin in school, an obsolete language."

"It's a good background to any language," Charles said.

They enjoyed their Eggs Benedict with coffee. Then they went back to bed. Charles said that they needed to work off some of the calories from breakfast.

Chapter 33

Andrea lived in a dream world. Her wedding and the night that followed had fulfilled all her expectations and more. Now, they were on their way to the airport in another limousine to a plane that would take them to Paris. Before they boarded, Charles said, "I should tell you that I have signed a new will in case something happens to me while we're away."

"I don't want to survive without you," she said.

"And I don't want to live without you, but let's not think about such unlikely things."

The airline steward ushered them into business class. The seats were wide and comfortable. Another steward brought them champagne. Charles showed Andrea how she could recline her seat and elevate the footrest so the seat turned into a daybed.

"When the lights go out, there'll be only a couple of hours for rest," he said and added, "We'll land in Paris at about three o'clock in the morning, our time. But over there, it will be late morning."

"That's amazing, but who needs to sleep when we can be in Paris."

"We'll be tired in the afternoon. You'll see. It's the jetlag."

"I've heard of it. I wonder how the pilots and the rest of the airline crew can cope."

"They never stay long enough in one place."

Andrea had just gone to sleep when the attendants began to serve breakfast. She opened her window shade and saw the sunshine outside her window and the ocean below.

"Look, Charles," she said. "I can see the coastline of France and ships below."

Charles stretched to look. "We'll fly over land shortly," he said.

Andrea followed the progress of the plane as it flew over the green countryside dotted with lakes, towns, and villages until she saw the metropolitan area of Paris. The plane began its descent, and she could see the buildings and the church steeples. The speaker announced the local time, and they moved their watches forward seven hours.

They landed at Charles De Gaulle Airport where the language on the loudspeakers was French. They went through passport controls and custom. Charles said the purpose of his visit was "pleasure," so she said the same and got a "Welcome to France" in return.

"We'll take the train to the city," Charles said. "It's quite far."

The train traveled many miles through the countryside before they saw any city buildings.

"Are you tired, darling?" Charles asked.

"No, I'm too excited to be tired."

"The corners of your mouth turn up as usual, pretty-face."

"You haven't called me that for a while."

"It's because I have so many other names for you now, but you still have a pretty face."

The conductor called out the names of the various stations in French. Charles listened intently until they had reached their destination.

"This is our stop," he said, and they disembarked the train. Everyone seemed to carry his or her own luggage, so Charles took one suitcase in each hand while Andrea carried a smaller bag. They put them down on the platform and Charles looked for a cabdriver to take them and their luggage to the hotel.

"Do you have French money? Andrea asked when they were seated in the cab.

"I have euros. You can buy them in U.S. banks. They're worth a little more than our dollar bills. Here're some euros for you in case you see something you want to buy."

"Thank you, Charles." Andrea looked at the bills and tucked them in her purse.

Charles paid the cabdriver with euros and they stepped out on Champs Elysees in front of the hotel.

"Look over there, darling." Charles said, turning Andrea slightly. "It's Arc de Triomphe. We'll look at it later, but first we're checking into our hotel."

"I'm thrilled to be here," Andrea said. With great anticipation, she followed Charles and the porter to their room.

"This is no bridal suite, honey, but it's the best I could get in the center of the city," Charles said.

"I like it, and best of all it's in Paris."

Andrea went to the bathroom to inspect. "It's beautiful," she said, "It has ceramics everywhere and gold faucets, and a hairdryer on the wall. How many euros are you paying for this?"

"You don't want to know, darling. Come and look at the view of the Champs Elysees."

"I want to walk on that famous avenue and sit on a sidewalk café and have lunch with you."

"That's what we'll do then. Do you want to take a shower first?"

"I think I'd rather wait."

"I need to shave," Charles said, touching his chin.

"Yes, I think you're right. Does your razor work here?"

"No, you need an adapter for that. I brought shaving cream and disposable razors."

"You'll get a kiss when you're done, honey."

The sidewalk café had a glass wall toward the avenue. They could see the crowds walking by on the wide sidewalk. Many of the women wore sport shoes with their office suits. How practical, Andrea thought. They probably have other shoes at the office. Charles spoke French with the waiter.

"I'm so impressed," Andrea said.

Charles repeated what the waiter had said—that it was unusual to hear an American speaking any French at all.

"We're not good at languages."

They ate the best soup that Andrea had ever tasted in her life.

"French cuisine is fantastic," she said. They finished the meal with a cappuccino, which was also fantastic.

"Do you suppose there are many tourists here at this time of the year?"

"Yes, there are. The Parisians themselves go on vacation in August and leave the city."

"I'm glad I brought sport shoes."

"Yes, we should both wear them tomorrow. What do you want to do now, darling?"

"Could we take a closer look at the Arc de Triomphe?" Andrea tried to make it sound French.

"Yes, of course."

"Is it a monument to something?"

"Yes, Napoleon Bonaparte had it built as a memorial to the French Army. Twelve wide avenues meet there."

"Can we go to the top?"

"No, I don't think so, unless you want to climb almost three hundred steps. There's no elevator."

They stood by the eternal flame under the arc. "The flame is dedicated to the Unknown Soldier of World War I," Charles said. "More than a million French soldiers died in that war."

"I didn't know. That's awful!" Other tourists crowded them, and they had to keep moving.

"We can take the subway or a cab to the Eiffel Tower," Charles said.

"Let's take a cab. We can ride the subway some other time."

"I read in a brochure that the Eiffel Tower is one-thousand feet high and that it was built for the 1889 World Exposition," Andrea said.

"Yes, and it was only going to be temporary, but now it has become the symbol of Paris." When they got out of the cab, they could see the tower.

"If we're going to take pictures of it, we have to do it from here," Charles said. "I want a picture of you with the tower in the background."

"We didn't take any pictures of the Arc."

"I'd rather do it when there aren't so many people around," Charles said. He focused the camera on her and said, "Smile, Mrs. Bordeaux."

They took the elevator to the top of the Eiffel Tower. From there, Charles pointed out the Cathedral of Notre Dame, the Church of Sacré Coeur, the Seine River, the Louvre Palace and Museum, and Place de la Concorde. "I hope to show you all those places," he said.

"I can see the Arc," Andrea exclaimed. "Paris is so beautiful."

"It's one of the most beautiful cities in the world. We're lucky that the weather is pleasant. It could be hot in August."

"It's perfect."

"You look a little tired, darling."

"Yes, I think the jetlag is getting to me."

"We can go back to the hotel and rest awhile before dinner."

"Yes, let's do that." Charles set the alarm on his wrist-watch and prepared to take a nap. Andrea dropped on the bed, and in the next moment, she was asleep.

The next thing she knew, Charles stood above her.

"Hi there, sleepyhead," he said.

"Oh, did I sleep too long?"

"It's dinner time."

"Your hair is wet. You've showered?"

"Yes."

"Then I'll do the same. It will wake me up."

"I'll go downstairs and reserve a table for us."

"Please take the key with you."

Chapter 34

Andrea dressed in her red lingerie, her red dress, and her diamond earrings. She was in Paris and wanted to look her best. When Charles returned to their room, he was pleased and complimented her.

"That takes me back to a certain cocktail party," he said, as he came up to her and kissed her. "I know what you have underneath," he teased. "I can't wait to undress you."

"We'll have a wonderful honeymoon in Paris."

"If it's anything like our wedding night, it will blow our minds."

"You're the best lover I could ever wish for, Charles. It might be due to your French genes."

He bent down and kissed the exposed parts of her breasts.

"The lights are going on in Paris. That's when the French go out to dine. You'll love Paris at night. It's the City of Lights," he said.

"It's so romantic."

After a marvelous dinner, they walked on the avenue and admired Arc de Triomphe in floodlights. They walked slowly with their arms around each other and stopped often to kiss. No one paid attention to them. Other lovers did the same. Charles said that Paris was also the City of

Love. Andrea looked in the store windows. She was curious about the Paris fashion.

"The prices look so high," she said.

"Yes, these boutiques are probably the most expensive. But nothing can beat your red dress," he said. "Not with you in it, or out of it for that matter. Can we go to our room now?"

"Yes, let's go." They thought of the same thing, being alone and making love in Paris. It did not disappoint them.

They woke up early in the morning and were ready for more sightseeing. It amazed Andrea how old the buildings were. The Cathedral of Notre Dame was more than 800 years old. It had taken 200 years to build. She asked if Charles' ancestors were Catholics.

"Yes, they were, but it has changed, at least in my branch of the family."

Musee Du Louvre had once been a royal palace. They followed the crowd to see the famous *Venus De Milo*, the Greek Goddess of Love that was created before year One.

"You're my Goddess of Love, Andrea," Charles said. "And you're a much more enjoyable creation."

They filed past the *Mona Lisa*, painted by Leonardo da Vinci. It was smaller than Andrea thought. The many tourists in line prevented them to stop and admire the painting. Andrea had seen many pictures of the famous Mona Lisa, but she loved the experience of seeing the original.

The next morning, Charles sent a text to Kathy asking about Nana and saying that they had enjoyed their first full day in Paris. Kathy answered, "Good, Nana's fine."

"Let me see," Andrea said. "That's amazing."

After breakfast, Charles suggested that they go to the *Musee d'Orsay* that housed impressionists and post-impressionists paintings. On the first floor, they saw the early-school impressionist artists Manet and Degas. On the upper floor, they saw paintings by Monet, Renoir, Cezanne, Gauguin, Van Gogh, and others. Andrea now understood the concept of impressionism. The artists created an impression of what they painted.

"I've seen a few paintings by the masters in the Chicago Art Museum," she said, "but this is unbelievable."

Dressed in shorts and sport shoes, they walked along the Seine and looked at what modern-day artists painted. Much of it was abstract art. Merchants sold reproductions of paintings depicting the famous landmarks in Paris, but Charles didn't want reproductions. He searched a long time before he decided on an original. He asked Andrea if she liked it and she did. The canvas portrayed a beautiful woman.

"I think she looks like you," he said.

"I'm glad she has clothes on."

He bargained for the best price. Finally, the money changed hands and the artist rolled up the canvas and handed it to Charles.

"We've to remember the artist's name in case he becomes famous," Andrea said.

"Yes, I have his name, but I buy art because I like it. It's the best way."

It was their last day in Paris. Tomorrow morning they would fly to Bordeaux.

"I feel melancholic," Andrea said. "I've fallen in love with Paris. Some day, we must return here."

"We may not be able to relive all aspects of our honeymoon."

"I'd be happy just to walk with you along the Seine," Andrea said.

At the Bordeaux airport, Charles rented a Citroen automobile.

"It feels good to be able to drive again," he said. "Would you like to go to the countryside and see some vineyards and scenery?"

"Yes, I'd love to. Do the Bordeaux wines come from here?"

"Yes, the authentic ones. I'd like to buy a case and take home."

"Was anyone in your family a winemaker?"

"I think they all were."

"Where did they live?"

"I'll show you if I can find it. I was here as a young man, and it might have changed a lot since then." He drove south toward the coast.

"Oh, Charles, it's so beautiful. Why did your ancestors leave?"

"Because of all the wars that France was in," he said, adding, "I think they should all have gone to California and become winemakers, but my branch of the family settled in Chicago."

"Where will we stay tonight?"

"I don't know. I think that's part of the fun, at least it was when I was young. We can stay at a country inn, or we can drive back to Bordeaux. I don't think we need reservations here, like we do in Paris."

"Do you feel a connection to this area?"

"In a way I do."

"Just the name Bordeaux makes me feel like we're connected."

"Sometime, we should go to Switzerland and Sweden and visit the areas where your ancestors came from."

"I'd like that. I never thought I would get the chance to do any of that."

Charles stopped to ask for direction to his ancestors' vineyard in the French language. With an excited look in his eyes, he turned to Andrea. "Can you believe it? The vineyard has the same name even though it changed owners."

They saw the rows of grapes growing on the hillside as they drove up to the buildings.

"This is unbelievable," Charles said, "I recognize this place."

"I'm so happy for you, and I'm just as excited."

He stepped out of the car, saying he would ask for the owners. She heard him introduce himself as Charles Bordeaux. A worker pointed to the manor house.

Charles came back to the car and drove up to the house. "I'll go first," he said. "Do you mind waiting in the car, honey?"

"Not at all. Good luck."

She saw Charles standing on the porch talking to a woman. He gave her his business card. The woman clasped her hands and invited him in. Charles pointed to Andrea. Then he came to get her.

"We're welcome to visit with the owner's wife," he said.

"Amazing! I don't think that would happen in America. How long ago was it that your ancestors lived here?"

"Nearly one hundred years ago."

The woman welcomed them like long-lost relatives. Andrea couldn't communicate with her, but Charles introduced her as his wife and translated for her.

"I'm getting better at this," he said

The visit ended with meeting the woman's winemaker husband and a tour of the winery. Charles explained to Andrea that they use the same process for making wine today as they did one-hundred years ago.

"The wine still has to age in oak barrels to make the best wines," he said.

When they left, Charles carried a case of wine. "It's a gift to us," he said. "I wanted to pay for it, but they wouldn't let me."

Andrea was overwhelmed. "This almost tops Paris," she said.

"I'm satisfied now," Charles said. "Wish I could tell my father that I've been here again after so many years."

"But you can tell your mother."

"Yes, she'll be happy to hear about our visit here."

"You don't look French, Charles."

"No, I probably look more like a Scotsman."

"And I look more like my father than my mother."

"I'd say you're a good combination of Swiss and Swedish genes, pretty-face. Shall we go back to Bordeaux?"

They took in at a hotel on Place Gambetta in the city's central square and celebrated the day by opening a bottle of Bordeaux. Charles told Andrea that the city of Bordeaux could boast of having the largest university campus in France.

The next day, they went to *Musee de Beaux-Arts* and looked at paintings by Rubens and Renoir. Andrea liked Renoir's paintings depicting French middle class. They admired the beautiful stained glass windows of the Cathedral of St. Andre. They walked along the River Garonne. They bought gifts to bring home to family members. They drove north to the mouth of the river and saw the Atlantic Ocean. The waves rolled endlessly toward the shore. "We could sail from here to America," Charles said.

"I'll never forget this vacation," she said. "I haven't enjoyed anything so much in my life."

Tomorrow, we'll return the car, fly to Paris, and catch our plane to Chicago," Charles said.

They were subdued as they drove back to their hotel in Bordeaux.

"Our honeymoon is over. I'll miss it," Andrea said.

"I'll miss it, too. It's been wonderful, but we've one more night."

They stopped to eat at a picturesque inn. As soon as they were back at the hotel, they began to kiss and were soon engaged in one more night of honeymoon pleasure.

In the morning, Charles checked his phone for the last time. "No messages," he said. "It means no problems either at the office or with Nana."

"I'm thankful for that," Andrea said. "It will be fun to get back home and tell everybody what we've seen. I haven't sent a single postcard. Now, it's too late, and I have euros left."

"You can use them up at De Gaulle. We can also shop tax free on the plane for perfume and chocolates."

"I should buy some Chanel No. 5 perfume for Jessica."

"It's a good idea. Buy some for yourself too."

Chapter 35

Jessica surprised them by being at O'Hare to meet them.

"I didn't think you should have to wait for a cab to take you home," she said.

"It feels good to have someone welcoming us."

"Jason is waiting in the car outside."

"So you're together again?" Andrea shrieked.

"Yes, Mom, we're together again."

"That's wonderful news. I'm so happy for you, sweetheart."

Andrea and Jessica sat in the back seat and talked all the way home. Charles sat up front with Jason, talking about what had happened lately in Chicago and in the States, especially the latest sports news.

"We didn't listen to the news and we didn't buy any newspapers. They have *USA Today* over there, but I only looked at the headlines a couple of times," Charles said.

"Have you heard about the flood in New Orleans?" Jason asked.

"I saw that hurricane Katrina hit the city, but I didn't know it flooded. Did the levy break?"

"Yes, it did. People are evacuating."

"That's too bad."

"Mom," Jessica said. "You got the job as a teacher's aide at my school if you still want it."

"I did? That's great. When can I start?"

"After Labor Day, but you have to let them know right away. There's another person waiting in the wings if you don't take it."

"I must give two weeks notice at the bookstore. What a dilemma. I really would like to work at a school. No evenings and no weekends."

"I'd like that," Charles said turning around. "Congratulations on being offered the position."

"Thanks honey."

"How's Nana?" Andrea asked Jessica.

"She's doing as well as can be expected. She'll be glad to see you again."

Jason turned into the driveway. He lifted the suitcases out of the trunk.

"What do you have in them, rocks?" he asked.

"Wine, I'll give you a bottle."

"I bet it's the good stuff."

"The best—aged Bordeaux made in France."

"Are you two ready for another wedding? Jessica has agreed to be my wife." Jason hugged her shoulders as he spoke. Jessica's eyes danced between them.

"That's so wonderful," Andrea said. "When?"

"It won't be until next year, Mom. Please keep it a secret until our engagement is announced."

"Of course, I'm so glad for you." She hugged them both, and Charles slapped Jason on the shoulders.

"We'll have to open a bottle or two of the wine and celebrate," he said.

"Home sweet home," Andrea said. "Are my flowers still alive?"

"Yes, Ernie has been doing a great job. I stopped by today to check on everything."

"I have a gift for you, Jessica, but I'll come over tomorrow."

"I'll be home."

"Thanks for picking us up," Andrea said and hugged her daughter. "I'm so glad you will marry Jason."

"Me too," Charles said. "Again, congratulations on your engagement, and thanks for the ride."

"It's good to be home," Andrea said. "Don't get me wrong, I've enjoyed every minute of our honeymoon."

"I know, but it's always good to return home," Charles said.

"Does it feel weird to you that your home is here?"

"Not weird, but if I had driven the car, I might have taken another exit by habit."

"It takes a while to get used to something new."

"You're the magnet that draws me here, darling."

"Should we unpack our suitcases?"

"I'm sure we'll wake up early tomorrow morning, so let's do it then, honey. I'd like to get out of my clothes and go to bed."

"I'm so happy about Jessica getting married," Andrea said, sleepily.

"You'll have another wedding to plan." They fell asleep at once in each other's arms.

As Charles had predicted, they woke up early. The clock showed 3:00 a.m. Their internal clocks were still on European time, and they were wide-awake.

"We might as well unpack our suitcases," Andrea said. She sorted her clothes and took almost everything to the laundry room. She took out bread from the freezer and made coffee. She would have to go shopping for fresh food. It was too early to make calls. She showered and washed her hair. It was still only four o'clock in the morning.

Charles set aside two bottles of wine for Jason and Jessica, and then took the rest to the basement. He unpacked his suitcase and separated the shirts and suits that would go to the cleaners. The rest he took to the laundry room.

They sat down in the kitchen and had coffee and toast. "This is our first breakfast for the day. We might have two more," Charles said. The sun began to rise and the birds sang outside their window. "It looks like it will be a beautiful day," he added.

"It's great to be up early in the summertime. I'll start the washing machine."

"I need to check my e-mails," Charles said. "I should let the kids know we're home."

"You do that, honey. Say hello to everyone from me."

Charles decided to go to the office early. "I'm sure there's work to do," he said, "but I'll be home early."

"I'm going to the bookstore later to give Bob notice about my resignation."

"Good luck! See you later, honey, I love you." He kissed her goodbye.

"I don't know which cleaner you use or how you want your shirts done."

"I'll take care of it," he said. "You shouldn't have to do that for me."

What a remarkable husband she had. No socks on the floor, and he takes his shirts to the cleaners.

She hummed as she dressed. Then she backed out her car and drove to the grocery store. She was home by seven, unpacked the groceries, moved the clothes from the washer to the dryer, and loaded the washer again. Then she went outside to look at her flowerbeds. Of course, they needed weeding. With her garden gloves on, she went to work pulling weeds.

She straightened her back and looked at her watch. It was eight o'clock, and she was hungry again. A glass of orange juice, fruit and cereal with yogurt tasted good. Charles had said that they would eat more than one breakfast. She already missed him as she ate by herself with the television as company. The news was mostly about New Orleans and the devastation that the hurricane had caused. Those poor people, she thought. They have lost everything.

Nana usually got up early, so Andrea decided to call her. Kathy answered and they had a long chat. Nana was looking forward to returning to her home.

"Your neighbor, Ernie Anderson, has visited her," Kathy said.

"Are you serious?

"Yes. It really perked her up. He'll probably be back because she needs to stay with me for another month or two."

"I didn't know they were that sweet on each other! Of course, Ernie is from Rockville and they've known each other for years. But how did he know that she was at your house?"

He had called her and when she didn't answer her phone, he called Mrs. Berg and she told him. Then he went to Mt. Sinai and visited Nana, and she must have told him she would be recuperating with me."

"I'm amused and amazed, but I'm happy for her. She told me that she had missed her chances to remarry. Perhaps it's not too late yet. Charles and I want to come and see her, and you, too, of course."

"Why don't you drive up here on Labor Day?"

"I think that's a good idea. Is Nana awake yet?"

"She's coming downstairs as we speak. I'm sure she wants to talk with you." Andrea clutched the receiver a little harder when her mother came on the phone.

"How're you, Nana?"

"I'm doing much better, but the doctor says it will take at least two months to recover completely. Kathy and Roger are so good to me, but eventually I'd like to be on my own again."

"You sound hopeful, Nana."

"I am. How was Paris?"

"It was wonderful. I'll tell you about France when we meet on Labor Day."

"I'm looking forward to it. Welcome home, honey."

Andrea called Nancy next and chatted with her for at least thirty minutes. Nancy was happy to have Nana nearby and glad that her girls got along so well with her. Andrea's earlier misgivings about her sisters were completely gone.

Chapter 36

Andrea needed another cup of coffee before going to the bookstore.

"Hello Bob!" she said cheerily as she entered the store. "I have this fantastic offer to work part time as a teacher's aide at Jessica's school, and I'm definitely resigning from my job here at the store as of today."

"I'm sorry to see you go, but you still have to work here part time for two more weeks from today," Bob said.

"Yes, I know, but do you think I could work afternoons only?"

"If you could do Labor Day and one more weekend, it would be alright," Bob said.

"Not on Labor Day. I'm going to see my mother then, but I can do one more weekend."

"I'll do my best to accommodate you."

"Thanks Bob. I'll let you know later today when I know more about my other job. I'll call you."

Andrea drove straight to Jessica's school.

"Miss Holm," the principal said as he greeted her.

"It's Mrs. Bordeaux now."

"I forgot. Congratulations on your marriage. We've been waiting for you. Can you accept the position we offered you? "

"Yes, if I don't have to work after one o'clock in the afternoon. I've another part-time job that I can't get out of for the next two weeks."

"You'll be working with morning kindergarteners and they get out at noon."

"Great, then I'll accept."

"Are you ready to sign a contract for the semester then, Mrs. Bordeaux?"

"Yes, I'm ready."

Andrea walked to the parking lot and looked back at the school building. The children would make it a lively place. She was elated. Finally, she had a dream job, and a dream husband to boot.

She got out her cell phone and dialed the number to the store.

"I'm just calling to say that our arrangement will work out just fine," she said to Bob.

"Alright, I'll see you Tuesday then at 2 p.m. Good luck with your new job."

"Thanks Bob."

Andrea drew a deep breath of relief. Surprisingly, Bob had not voiced any objections. Everything had gone smoothly. She didn't think Charles would mind her temporary heavy workload because in just two weeks all her weekends would be free.

Next, she called Jessica and blurted out, "Hi, honey, I got the job at your school."

"Wonderful, Mom, congratulations."

"I'll be working two jobs for the next two weeks, but I can do it."

"Are you doing Kindergarten in the morning and the bookstore in the afternoon?"

"Yes, that's what I'll do, but I was wondering if I can come and see you?"

"Yes, of course, Mom."

Andrea happily carried the two bottles of wine and the small bottle of perfume to Jessica's door.

Jessica opened the perfume at once and applied some on her arm.

"Chanel No. 5, it must be expensive, but what a wonderful fragrance," she said sniffing it. She picked up a wine bottle and studied the label.

"It's hard to believe that this wine comes from Charles' ancestral vineyard. Thank you so much. We'll save it for our engagement party. I couldn't wait to tell you. No one else knows."

"So all Jason needed was a little time to think about how much you mean to him. I knew he would come around."

"I think he got nervous when he heard about your wedding. After you had left on your honeymoon, he came and apologized. When I accepted, we fell into each other arms, and he proposed. Making up was so sweet. We decided not to tell anyone until you got home."

"I'm so glad for the happy ending. Charles and I are going to Kathy's on Labor Day. Do you think you and Jason could come along? It would give you a chance to spring the news about your engagement."

"I'd love to tell Nana face-to-face, but I'll have to ask Jason."

"You do that, honey. Then just give me two weeks to finish up my job at the book store, and I'll throw an engagement party for all your friends."

"That would be great, Mom. Jason and I are already planning to go to Sweden and Denmark on our honeymoon."

"You'll love it. Where did his ancestors come from?"

"He says he's a concoction of nationalities, but he'll be glad to honor my heritage."

When Charles came home, Andrea couldn't wait to tell him that she had signed a contract with the school, and that she had to work two part-time jobs for the next two weeks, but only one weekend.

"I'm proud of you," he said.

"But you'll have to manage on your own."

"I'll muddle through if you can, honey."

"I'll probably be coming home later than you from work."

"Then I'll make dinner, or we can go out to eat."

"We're invited to Kathy's for a Labor Day cookout. Jessica and Jason might come along. Do you feel like driving up there, honey?"

"Sure, by then we should be over our jetlag, but I've something to tell you, darling. Today, we settled the accident insurance case."

"And how did it go?"

"I didn't want to tell you earlier, but the young man who caused the accident had let his insurance lapse. He attends college and lacks assets. He also has student loans. We could have garnered his future earnings, but I didn't want to do that. He lost his car, and his insurance premium will be sky high, so it's punishment enough. I'm covered for uninsured motorists, and the whole thing will be applied to my insurance. You'll be compensated, honey."

"I do admire you for being lenient on the young student. You're a good person, and I love you."

"It's good to have that behind us. Now we can go forward and reap the rewards of our accidental encounter."

"Something good may also have come from Nana's heart attack. Ernie has visited her, and it looks like they are sweet on each other. Can you believe it, at their age?"

"I've seen it happen before, so why not? People can fall in love even after the age of 70 and 80."

"I've seen it too, but I didn't think it would happen to my mother."

"Nana will be good as new if she can look forward to something special in her life."

"She's planning to move back to her home, but perhaps Ernie will move in with her, or she'll come and live with him. Just think, Nana might live next door to us!"

"Time will tell, darling."

Charles had brought home a copy of the *Chicago Tribune*, and they read about the devastating flood in New Orleans caused by hurricane Katrina. They turned on the television, watched and listened. How could everything go so wrong? Would the historic city ever be the same?

"We're incredibly lucky," Andrea said. "I feel so sorry for those people."

He yawned. "I'm getting sleepy," he said. "Do you want to take a nap with me, darling?"

"Yes, I do. I feel that I've accomplished a lot today."

"So do I, but we started early."

"My car made a funny noise when I drove home," she said.

"Tomorrow, we'll go to my car dealer and pick out a new car for you, and don't protest, darling. You need a dependable car when you're working two jobs."

"You're too good to me, honey."

They lay down on top of the bed with their clothes on. Charles spooned his wife and put his arms around her as she closed her eyes.

"I'm so happy," she said.

"I couldn't be happier than I am right now," he said and gave her a squeeze.

The Author's Comments

When I began writing this story several years ago, I did so because all the novels I read were about young people. It was as if no one over the age of 50 had any romantic feelings left in their bodies or could fall in love. In reality, it seemed to me that there were plenty of men and women who formed new relationship and married again after they had been widowed or divorced. So why not write about them?

I was so optimistic about a successful novel that I contacted a big publisher about my manuscript. It took about six months to get an answer, but then I was encouraged to do some rewriting and resubmit. The problem was that I had no clue about how to do the rewrite.

After much procrastinating, I contacted a very kind and experienced writer with many books published and received some good advice. Sally, I'm sorry it took so long for me to follow your advice. At the time, it was hard for me to put down someone else's ideas on paper. I didn't have much in common with my main character, and somehow, I had to get into Andrea's head and understand her.

I gave up and went back to writing nonfiction books and two historical-fiction novels. Occasionally, I picked up the mothballed contemporary novel and tried to make sense of it. I read chapters from it for our critique group and received many positive comments.

After several nonfiction books that required much research, I needed a respite from the time-consuming work and asked myself if I could do something about that novel of mine written in MS Word 2003 before the file became totally obsolete.

With fresh eyes, I rewrote, edited, and polished the story until I thought it was acceptable. A friend in my critique group read the script. Thank you, Mary. You caught a few errors and pointed out what I needed to clarify. Since then, I have made changes. Anyone who has written a book knows that when you think you are done, you are not really done. It always needs more work. I received much needed help from a family member with the final proofreading. In the end, I am the one responsible for any oversights. Finally, here it is! My dream of a big publisher has faded. It would be much too late to resubmit. The fictitious story still takes place in 2005. I like to think that my characters have lived ten years of marital bliss!

It was fun to make some of the secondary characters Swedish, Danish, and Irish, and having the honeymooners fly to Paris, because I love Paris too.

Thank you for reading my first and probably last contemporary novel. I would be ever so grateful if you would comment on the story on one of the sites that carries the book, or on my blog.

About the author

Lilly Setterdahl was born in Sweden, but lives in Illinois. So far, she has authored 16 books pertaining to the Swedish immigration to America, and two historical novels about the Titanic. She has received many awards and positive reviews. Lilly credits her interest in Swedish immigration history to her late husband, Lennart. Some of her titles are still available online.

Lilly's next book will be a historical-fiction immigration novel.

More about the author and her books on:
http://lillysetterdahl.blogspot.com

Made in the USA
Lexington, KY
04 February 2017